The 7th Semester

I0664678

Priyam Kumar

DIAMOND BOOKS

SMS New Book at
9911044500 for Alert

ISBN : 978-81-288-3534-6

© Author

Publisher : **Diamond Pocket Books (P) Ltd.**
X-30, Okhla Industrial Area, Phase-II
New Delhi-110020

Phone : 011-40712200

E-mail : sales@dpb.in

Website : www.diamondbook.in

The 7th Semester
By - *Priyam Kumar*

Dedication

To my grandparents,
my Dadaji - Dadiji & Nanaji - Naniji,
who have cared for me all my life
and brought me up with values which define me.

Acknowledgement

In any story, its characters not merely shape the story, but also breathe life into it. Many people, directly or indirectly influenced me, and thus, this story turned out to be what it is. I might not be able to mention all the names, but the ones I might have missed out, will surely understand.

First of all I would like to thank my *Dadiji* – who, like a beacon, is a great pillar of strength and a constant source of inspiration, not just to me, but our entire family.

I would like to thank my father, Rajiv Gupta, who always encouraged me to dream and helped this dream come true. I know I will not be as good a writer as him, but I am trying.

My Mother, Neelam,who held my finger when I took my first step, loves and cares for me more than anyone else. My brother, Kartikeya, for his innocence, that I know, is the essence of my life.

To my cousins Sarina, Rohan, Mohit, Shivani, Eesha, Govinda, and especially my two sisters Vidisha and Mahima, whom I have grown up with, and who have always supported me.

To my aunt, Vibha Gupta, who relentlessly works for the millions of rural folk living in the mud huts and is a true model of patriotism for me in today's world.

To all my friends in school, college and Infosys,who have always stood by me — through thick and thin. And, to all my teachers, who have taught me many valuable lessons of life besides studies.

My special thanks to Dr. Jaideep Chadha for his invaluable professional advice.

To Vikas and Sonia, for their continuous encouragement and vital inputs.

To my brother-in-law, Mayank, the first to read and appreciate my work.

I would greatly like to thank the publishers of this book, as they realized the intrinsic value of a story, which means more than anything else to me. This, being my first baby, I hope this venture to be a success to gain all the love and admiration from the world around me.

Lastly, I would like to thank the Almighty for everyone and everything I have.

– Priyam Kumar

Prologue

'Harsh, where the hell are you?'

Suhaas felt cheated, for none of his friends had arrived before him on the day of his college farewell. It was three in the afternoon and he felt that he had taken the foolish decision to come alone by a cab. If he had come with his friends, he wouldn't have to call his friend Harsh on his cell phone.

'I talked to the others. They won't come before seven and I am in no mood to be alone. Find someone to talk to. I told you not to reach college early. Had you car-pooled with me and the others, we would have enjoyed together.'

'You don't need to preach me today. I'll do something for time-pass,' said Suhaas and hung up.

The farewell function was to start around seven. Suhaas knew his friends wouldn't arrive before time. He had informed Harsh to tell his other buddies to reach college before three. He knew that Prakash must have changed the plan at the last second, so that they all came late, dressed up like film stars for the rest of the college to see.

Suhaas cursed himself for reaching early. Only a few students were present in the college. The food stalls were to be arranged later. Even the tents hadn't been set up. Suhaas sighed and sat under a tree. He looked at the college gate in the faint hope that someone known would enter the campus.

Just then, a pretty young girl entered the gate. Suhaas stared as she stood next to him. He had never seen this girl in the college before. He was even more amazed when she spoke to him.

'It's three p.m. I thought this was the official time, the final year students were supposed to reach college.'

'I am sorry. I don't know you,' asked Suhaas.

'I am not from this college. This is my friend's college. I thought she would be here by now.'

'She won't come early, the actual function starts at seven,' I said.

'Drat! Now I'll be bored for hours,' she said.

'Are you from Delhi?' asked Suhaas.

'Yes.'

'Me too.'

For a whole long minute, they did not talk.

'You have must be having a story to tell,' she said.

Suhaas laughed.

'This is Ikatram Institute of Technology in Gurgaon, Haryana. It is named so that professors can proudly abbreviate it as I.I.T. This is not some top notch Engineering college with something exclusive to tell. I landed here because I got a low AIEEE ranking. It's an ordinary college with ordinary people.'

'I'd listen to anything than get bored,' said the girl.

'I don't have much to offer.'

'What does your story have?'

Suhaas pondered for a few seconds.

'Well, it has love, struggle, friends and blunders,' said Suhaas.

'Then tell,' the girl insisted.

Suhaas had to talk to someone anyway. So he told his story from the very beginning —

THE FIRST SEMESTER

As my bus neared my college, I saw a single huge building with bold letters displaying "Ikatram Institute of Technology." This was the first day of my college life.

I stopped in front of the main gate with the others who crowded near the guard, who let each person in – one by one.

'I-Card?' the guard asked the boy in front of me.

I freaked out. I was so stupid. I simply forgot to carry my Identity Card.

'I don't have it with me right now,' replied the boy.

'Then you can't get in,' the guard thundered.

'But today is my first day. Please, let me in,' pleaded the boy.

'NO! NO ONE GETS IN WITHOUT AN IDENTITY CARD,' shouted the guard.

The boy stamped his foot on the ground and stood dejected on one side.

Everyone showed their I-Cards and entered the gates. A hand tugged at my shirt. I turned back and saw a beautiful girl smiling at me.

'What's the problem?' she asked.

'I don't have my I-Card.'

'That's no prob. Here, look at my I-Card.'

Her I-Card was in a red plastic frame with a strap, which she was supposed to hang around her neck.

'Just stand near the wall and make sure the guard is not looking at you. He will be busy checking the other I-Cards anyway. Just wait. And, tell that boy who doesn't have the I-Card to stay there too,' the girl added and went across to the guard. She showed her I-Card and went inside.

I didn't know what she was about to do. I hurried to the boy who had been yelled at and talked to him.

'Listen. Just stand near the wall with me. I will try to get you in.'

We walked towards the wall and looked at the guard. A tide of students flooded the entrance and the guard didn't get time to even look up as he was busy checking I-Cards.

'Good,' I said to myself.

'Here!' came the girl's voice from the other side of the wall.

I put my ear close to the wall and listened carefully.

'I am throwing the plastic case in the air. Catch it and fool the guard with it,' the girl said.

She threw the case over the wall and I caught it by the strap.

'How is that going to help you?' the boy next to me asked.

I didn't reply and hung the strap around my neck with the case in my shirt pocket.

As the guard saw me, he asked me for my I-Card. I acted like I was trying to get my I-Card out of my pocket. I flashed the back of the red plastic case.

'Okay. You have a card. Now get in,' the guard said and I entered the gate.

The girl was standing near the wall, surrounded by the small plant pots. I came near her and gave back her plastic case.

'Thanks,' I said.

'No problem,' she replied and threw the plastic case over the wall.

'Hey,' we heard the boy shout outside the wall.

'Use the case as I did,' I shouted to the boy outside.

'The guard is pretty strict,' the girl said.

'The guard won't fall for that again,' I said to the girl.

'There are lots of students right now. We came early. He doesn't have time to look at each and every card carefully,' she told me.

'How come the card is with you now? It wasn't there before,' the guard asked the boy.

'It was in my bag,' he replied and the guard hurriedly swept him inside the gate.

'I have such bad manners. I didn't even ask your name,' I apologized to the girl.

'My name is Aakriti,' she grinned.

'Hey, you didn't ask my name,' I blurted when she was turning to leave.

'We are in the same college. I will know it,' smiled the girl and left.

'Wow,' I said to myself.

'Hi,' said the boy without the I-Card.

'Hey. You did it. The guard believed you,' I said.

'Yeah, nice girl! What's her name?'

'Aakriti. But she didn't ask mine.'

'Well, I am Harsh.'

'My name is Suhaas,' I introduced myself, and we walked towards the college ground.

All the students assembled near a stage that trembled under the weight of the lecturers and other faculty members.

The only man who was all charged up was the principal. I closed my eyes and my thoughts drifted towards Aakriti.

She had a killer smile. She was very pretty, fair and really cute. I searched the girls' line for Aakriti but couldn't find her.

'Look. That's Jaggu,' said Harsh and pointed at a tall muscular senior who stood in a different line at the other end.

'What about him?' I asked.

'Be careful. He does the worst ragging and is a real *Gunda*.'

Jaggu — the name did seem mean and so did the person.

'Harsh, don't be scared,' I solaced him.

'Ragging is an offence and those who will be caught shall be severely punished,' lectured the principal.

All the seniors glared at us and gave a malicious grin. I gulped and felt like a tiny lamb surrounded by lions.

'In the end, we welcome all our first year students,' summed up the principal and left the stage.

My stream was Electronics and Communication Engineering or ECE. Computer Science Engineering was CSE, Information Technology Engineering was simply IT and Mechanical Engineering was ME.

'We are in the same college bus,' Harsh told me.

'It would have been better if we were in the same classroom,' I told him as we talked in the canteen during the break, on the first day.

'If they reshuffle the classes, we might be together in the same class,' said Harsh as he ate his sandwich.

'When we get on the bus in the afternoon, the seniors are going to take a really good bite out of you.' said Harsh.

I could only imagine what would happen.

In the afternoon, I boarded the college bus with Harsh. I sat with Harsh, behind the driver and with a professor. The deadliest row was the last row. Six fourth year students sat there and thus it was named F-row after the fourth year gang.

The fourth year boys sat in their seats comfortably and took out a pack of cards. I saw them taking out an empty paint can lying on the back steps of the bus as the back door was always bolted. They upturned the empty can and used its flat bottom as a table. As they started shuffling the cards, I looked at Harsh.

'Hey. I think they are in no mood for ragging today,' I said to Harsh.

'Don't be too hopeful. Let them finish their game. Then, we will see,' Harsh said to me.

Sure enough, as soon as they finished the game, the unshaven boy gave a message to the boy sitting in front of him. He passed the message forward and finally reached a boy in the fourth row.

Fifteen minutes later, someone tugged at my shirt from below. I looked down to see a girl on a seat who told me to go to the last row. I slowly walked over to the last row and faced the fourth year gang.

'Sit on the edge of the top step,' said the bearded fourth year student.

I parked my butt on the edge and screamed. I had sat on a nail.

'Yeah! You'll have to adjust with it.'

I cursed him under my breath and that was a big mistake. The bearded boy heard it.

'How dare he!' he shouted and got up.

Just then, another fourth year student held his hand.

'Sit down, man,' said the fourth year to the boy who was still standing.

I saw this fourth year boy. He wore a grey cap and a black shirt with jeans. He had a chain around his neck and beads in his ears. He seemed too young to be in the fourth year.

'Did you hear what he said to me?' said the bearded boy.

'He said it to me boss. I was staring at him. I'll deal with him later. Forget it,' replied the capped fourth year boy.

'Sing a Hindi song and use the 'F-word' in every sentence. Start!' boomed the bearded boy.

'I don't know any, sir' I lied, trembling.

'If you don't cooperate, I'll punch you in the face.'

'Hey there's a first year,' said the capped boy, pointing to someone.

'Learn something and then come. You are a bore,' said the bearded boy.

I gladly got up and walked to Harsh.

'That was quick. What did they make you do?' Harsh asked me.

'They wanted me to sing the song. But that fourth year with the grey cap saved me. Someone else has gone,' I told Harsh and he smiled.

The next morning, as the fourth year capped student got down the bus, I talked to him.

'Hi,' I said.

'Hi.'

'Sir, I am thankful to you. You saved me from ragging.'

He looked at me and laughed.

'I am not a fourth year student, friend. I am a fresher like you. Girish, Mechanical Engineering stream,' he introduced himself.

'Why didn't they rag you?'

Girish smiled and patted me on my back.

'I am good at cards so they wanted me to give them company. They told me to have fun while they did the ragging. I had no choice. Hence,' Girish said.

'Sorry, but I got to go,' said Girish and rushed to the college building.

I reached my classroom and saw the students already seated in their chairs. It meant I was late. The professor saw me.

'Where are you going?' he asked.

'To my seat sir.'

'Is it your habit to defy the authorities?'

I did not know what to say and just opened my mouth when he bellowed.

'YOU ARE TEN MINUTES LATE! 600 SECONDS! DO YOU HAVE ANY IDEA WHAT THAT FIGURE IS IN MATHEMATICAL TERMS?'

As I opened my mouth again to speak, he spoke up again.

'You shall stand in your seat for the rest of the lecture. If you try to sit for even one second, I will have to suspend you for a week.'

'But sir, that's harsh,' a student protested.

I looked at the student.

'Well, you will meet the same fate if you don't shut up!' the professor told the student.

'Sir, I'm sorry,' I said.

After the class, I met the student who defended me.

'Thanks,' I said.

'He's an old pea brain. Don't take him too seriously.'

'My name is Suhaas.'

'I am Prakash.'

When we stepped outside the class, we met Harsh and Girish.

'We should all go to the malls on our own,' said Prakash.

'Fine,' we all agreed. We walked to the main road and took an auto to the bus terminal. From there, we took a bus to IFFCO square. And from there, we walked to the mall.

'Let's watch a movie,' said Harsh.

'I won't,' I said.

'Will you be fine?' asked Prakash.

I nodded and they went to watch the movie. I saw a bookshop and entered it. I checked out the various titles. I found an interesting one - *How to get back at your ex and current traitor* interesting. I was totally engrossed in it when someone across the book rack sneezed. I looked up to face the cover of *'This Life and Beyond.'*

'I think you've got cold or something,' I ventured.

The second she lowered the book, I smiled with delight.

'Thanks for your concern, Suhaas,' said Aakriti.

'How do you know my name?' I asked.

'I told you yesterday. I'll find out.'

'Whom did you ask?'

'I just know it. It's no big deal,' said Aakriti.

We left the shop and talked.

'So?' I blurted.

'Don't get the wrong idea. It's just a usual habit for me to find out who's new,' Aakriti said.

'New?'

'Yeah, I mean I'd like to know juniors,' Aakriti said.

Shoots! She was a senior. She looked younger than me!

'So you are in —?' I asked.

'Final year,' Aakriti replied promptly.

Final year! What did God do, freeze her in time till I entered the college? Maybe, selecting this college was my best decision ever.

'You have no decency,' she quipped.

'What?'

'You didn't even buy me an ice cream.'

So, we stepped outside the shop and I bought two cones.

'So what would you like to eat?' I asked her.

'Whatever you can afford,' she mocked jokingly.

Time flew like a super fast AirForce jet. Or maybe it froze. All the while we talked and ate, I looked at her. I saw her eating cheap sandwich and chips with delight. She got furious when she found the cheese less than she had expected. She didn't look bad when her cheeks and the tip of her nose became red with anger. She looked cute, like I had said before.

'Hey, what's up?' she asked.

I blinked my eyes and looked around. I didn't realize that I was staring at her.

'Have I got something on my lips?' she asked.

Her lips, as I looked at them, were rosy and red. If only I could....

Like a song from hell, my cell phone rang. I looked at the number. It was Prakash. How much I hated Prakash at that moment. Aakriti wiped her lips with a tissue to check nothing was there. Her lips, I wondered again.

The phone kept ringing. The fool, I thought. Prakash had this annoying habit of giving missed calls like most people, but at that very moment of bliss, he felt like actually calling me.

I picked up the phone.

'What's so urgent?' I asked Prakash.

'The movie is over and we are meeting you at the ground floor,' he informed.

'You could have messaged that Prakash, why did you call?'

'Why do you sound so livid, is there someone with you?' Prakash asked.

Aakriti got up from her seat. Maybe I didn't look as cute as her when I was angry. Whatever be the reason, she waved me goodbye and disappeared.

'Well?' Prakash persisted.

'No, I am all alone.'

After two weeks or so, classes went on as usual. But on one fine day:

'Very good, you are progressing,' said the Math Prof.

I smiled. It seemed to me like everything was going right for me – first Aakriti, and now this Math.

'You were bad before. Now you are worse. You are approaching towards minus infinity from 0 in the matters of performance. That is a colossal improvement, though only in the negative direction,' the professor smirked.

'I am sorry,' I said.

'Did you revise?' the Prof. grilled me.

Now I could not refuse him point blank. I had to make some excuse.

'I did sir. In fact I almost did revise everything, except for this particular derivation.'

'This is the only thing I wrote yesterday, boy. It was an hour long derivation.'

'Sir, actually...' I started when he cut in.

'Stop making excuses.'

I controlled my temper and broke the chalk in my hand. I walked back to my seat.

'I have an announcement to make,' said the professor.

'What?' the students asked.

'On Monday, your sessional exams will commence,' he said.

'What's the first exam?' I asked.

'Your favourite,' the professor grinned and left the class.

As the bell rang, everyone left the class. Outside, there was a notice on the wall.

'It's the whole exam schedule,' said Prakash.

'Math,' I cried and nearly fainted. Prakash and Harsh came to my rescue to prevent me from falling.

'Relax, okay,' said Harsh.

'Forget about this, let's go to the canteen,' suggested Prakash.

I went to the canteen with them. I sat at a table while they headed for the food counter.

'I have two extra juices. An apple and an orange, besides my pineapple,' said Aakriti as she suddenly appeared from nowhere.

'Thanks, you never fail to surprise me,' I said as I took one. I looked at the other two.

'Well, these are for my three friends, who did not turn up.'

I looked towards the food counter and found Prakash and Harsh looking at me.

'So where are your friends? The ones with whom you came to the mall. They can have these juices,' she asked.

The two gave me a questioning look.

'Let's go and sit under that tree,' I said as I spotted a tree in the small garden adjoining the canteen.

'Our sessional exams are coming up,' I said.

'Ours too.'

'So, what is your favourite subject?'

'Mathematics,' she replied instantly.

I felt as if something choked my windpipe. I felt woozy in my stomach.

'I meant subjects related to your department,' I said.

'I am talking about engineering mathematics. One of your subjects,' cleared Aakriti.

Now, where was the paper bag for me to vomit in?

'I just love people who are good in mathematics. I was good at it and I would be impressed to find out a boy equally good at it,' she said.

Damn it! This was a shocker.

'Mathematicians are good at science and economics both,' she said.

We talked a bit and then she left for her class. The moment she left, Harsh and Prakash hopped over to me.

'What was all that about?' pounced Harsh.

'Yeah, how do you know each other?' Prakash asked.

'He met her on the first day of college. He didn't have his ID. She smuggled him in,' unfolded Harsh.

'Clever, nice,' said Prakash happily.

'Stop talking, guys,' I said.

'Why?' asked Prakash.

'Aakriti likes guys who are good at mathematics,' I said to myself.

'Which you suck at,' reminded Prakash.

I knew that. I thought I would study well for it. But as it turned out, for the next two days I had to be out of town with my parents. I had no time to study at all.

As I sat in the exam I was really terrified. I didn't know what to do. But I was quite amazed at how fortunes had turned in my favour. The paper was objective, meaning it was a multiple choice question paper. A scientific calculator appeared on my desk from nowhere, which raised a few questions in my head.

Why would I need it? Even if there were any calculations involved, I had no idea about them. And who passed it? I looked around to check when I saw Prakash. He looked at me and then looked down. He looked at me and mouthed 'look down.' I looked at the calculator. On the screen were displayed '1+4'. What was I supposed to do with 5? Oh my god! The answer of the first question was answer number four. I looked at Prakash happily and he gave me thumbs up. As soon as I marked the answer in my answer sheet, the boy sitting ahead of me said 'pass.'

I obeyed immediately and passed it to the boy in the adjoining row. He passed it to the boy ahead of him.

I had no calculator of my own and neither did I know any of the answers. But in the end, I was getting all the right answers to all my questions. So, all is well that ends well.

I imagined the math professor scratching his head in bewilderment.

So the week after my sessionals were over (and as the other papers I actually knew well enough, though none were as scoring), I proudly displayed my perfect score in the math paper to Aakriti.

'Wow. Excellent,' beamed Aakriti in admiration.

'So, are you impressed?' I asked.

'Very.'

'So, are you taking part in the Mr. and Ms. Fresher competition?'

'What is that?'

'It's a part of the fresher party. To welcome the first year students,' she explained.

'It must be a bore.'

'Whatever suits you, I am performing anyway,' she informed.

'What?' I was all ears.

'I am performing a dance with my group, just before the final round,' she said.

If Aakriti was performing, I was ready to see the whole show.

I was least interested in the fresher party. I wanted to see Aakriti's performance. Two hours had gone by but she was nowhere to be seen.

'I'll come back after some time,' I informed Prakash and Harsh and proceeded to the juice counter. I was roaming around the counter when I heard the announcement.

'And now, before the final round, we have this evening's last performance,' the host announced.

'This is it,' I thought.

'Hey!' someone shouted from behind.

I turned.

'Led by Aakriti and her group,' the host declared and the audience applauded.

I witnessed my worst nightmare – Jaggu.

'Hey you junior! You haven't introduced yourself. Bad manners,' he said as he stood blocking my path, with his friends.

It was hard to show courage and effrontery when I knew I was going to be battered. I had to see Aakriti's performance. But, he gave me no chance.

I turned in the other direction to run, when his fellow goons caught me. Jaggu punched me right in the face.

'Move your body now, shake your body now,' echoed the music in the background.

Meanwhile my whole body shook as Jaggu struck an upper cut, whammed a blow right along the side of my face, kicked me a few times, and then struck me again. By the time Jaggu beat me to pulp and left with his friends, the drumming in my head was the most dominating sound, whereas the music of the dance faded away. The last thing I heard before becoming unconscious was the applause of the audience.

'Wake up!' shouted someone as I was slowly gaining consciousness.

'Hey, who is it?' I asked, unable to figure it out in the dark.

'It's me, Aakriti,' reassured the voice.

Her beautiful face shimmered in the silvery moonlight as the clouds in the sky parted.

'What happened to you? Looks like a car ran over you,' she said.

'Worse. It was Jaggu.'

'Here,' she said and placed a napkin on my eye.

'Ouch,' I screamed in pain as she tried to hold me still.

'I just puffed some air in it. It's hot. But your left eye is sore. So, this will help.'

I looked at her. Maybe she cared for me or it was just sympathy. For whatever reason it may be, I didn't want her to leave me.

'Is the party over?' I asked her, realizing that I had lost all track of time.

'It's dinner time. Everything else is over,' she said.

'What happened to your performance?'

'You didn't see my performance?'

I felt slightly ashamed.

'Jaggu bashed me just before your performance. Henceforth,' I finished.

'Let me just find Jaggu. I'll teach him some manners.'

She was ready to deal with a bully just for me. I was touched.

'Okay. I am fine. I can have dinner now,' I said.

'But you are all hurt and bruised. You shouldn't even move,' she said.

'I feel perfect. Go and enjoy your dinner. I'll take care of myself,' I said.

'But,' she started and I interjected.

'Go.'

She left and I limped my way to the dining area. Stalls of *food* and *chaat* were lined-up all along the fence of the college ground. I limped my way to the table where Prakash and Harsh were having their dinner.

'What happened to your face?' asked Harsh.

'Did you get smashed by a truck or something?' asked Prakash.

I took Prakash's glass of juice and raised it in the air.

'It was the best night of my life,' I said, smiling like a zombie.

Two months after the fresher party, I talked about Aakriti with Prakash.

'I think I am in love with Aakriti,' I said.

'Obviously, that is the only name that comes to your lips every day,' quipped Prakash.

We were in the computer lab, unable to figure out what the program on the board meant. But I guess Prakash did not know the program running on my mind.

'Your case is hopeless,' sympathized Prakash.

'Why do you think so?' I asked.

'She is three years older than you. She may already be having a boyfriend of her own age and might reject you.'

But I knew what I had to do. I had to tell her.

The day I had thought of proposing to Aakriti, I could think of nothing else. I could think of nothing else but her. I had to spell it out; I could hold it in my heart no longer. I knew that Aakriti stayed in Janakpuri, West Delhi and I in South. But the only time to talk to her was in her bus. I could have proposed to her during the lunch break or before her classes.

As soon as the bell rang to end the last lecture, I jumped over my desk and ran out of the classroom door towards the buses. As I passed by my bus, Girish stared out of the bus window. Before I could evade his vision, he looked at me directly in the eye and asked:

'Where to, man? Are you not coming with us?'

I turned back and saw Harsh and Prakash standing, waiting for an answer. I looked at Girish.

'I am going in the West Delhi bus,' I informed.

'You are not going home?' Girish asked.

'I have some work in Punjabi Bagh. I'll go home from there,' I clarified.

Girish looked disappointed. Harsh and Prakash seemed surprised.

As soon as I stepped into the bus, my nose caught the rosy scent of ladies' perfume.

Expectedly, it led me to Aakriti.

I went up to her seat and said softly, 'Hey Aakriti.'

'Hi,' Aakriti said cheerily.

'I am not on this route. I had to go somewhere so I got on this bus,' I lied.

'Wow. We have a lot of things to talk about then, don't we? I am glad,' she said.

That was a positive sign.

'Sit,' Aakriti said.

We talked a bit and I told her about my day.

'You had a terrible day,' she expressed.

She showed me her project file, a spiral-bound assembly of pages. I knew she was a computer student and there was a huge computer language coding in her file.

'Looks great,' I commented.

'That's what my guide professor said. He couldn't believe that I could do the coding alone,' she said.

'I have to tell you something,' I told her.

'What?' she asked. My statement hung in mid air.

'It's like, you know, I can't say it well,' I said unclearly. People say it's easy to propose and say 'I like you' or 'I love you' when you like someone. Maybe it is. But very few dare to say it. At least I did.

'Suhaas,' said Aakriti sternly.

'What?'

'Say it,' she said and held my hand.

'I love you,' I spurted out.

I looked at Aakriti. She didn't smile. I thought she would slap me, or at least looked shocked. She was unperturbed.

'Aakriti?' I asked.

'Oh my god, not again,' she said to herself.

I was baffled by her response as all I expected was a simple 'yes' or 'no' to the words I had not said. But she didn't give a straight answer. She was a girl after all.

'You misunderstood our friendship,' she said.

'No,' I said as an automatic response.

'Yes, you did. I hear these words every year,' she said.

She said everything so casually as if she was talking about her favourite food.

'Besides, I know whom I like. I already have a boyfriend. Sorry, Suhaas,' she said and patted on my back.

I felt sick, nauseous, but knew that nothing would come out. I should have never expected a 'yes'.

The bus stopped for some students to get down. I rushed to the gate and quickly descended the steps. I could barely walk another step. Someone behind me dragged me ahead. But neither did I care or have the strength to look back.

'You need to express your feelings. I brought you home when you proposed to Aakriti in the bus, remember? I deserve to be a part of your sorrow or your anger or both,' said Harsh.

It had been a week after my meeting with Aakriti and I was in the canteen. I was dumped by the girl I liked. I had thought she might say 'yes'. But my heart was broken when she said 'no'.

Harsh had followed me that day into Aakriti's bus. He sat in the row behind me and heard my half-baked proposal to Aakriti and her reply. He had got down from the bus after me and dragged me to an auto. He took me home.

'I knew she had a boyfriend,' said Prakash.

'You should have told me, dork,' I said.

After lunch, Harsh went to his classroom. Prakash and I went to ours. Just after a few minutes into our lecture, the principal and few people entered the classroom.

'The chairman,' said the principal, pointing to a short fat man, 'has an announcement to make.'

The chairman spoke in a rather heavy voice.

'Keeping in mind the discipline we want to inculcate in our students and the needs of the market, we need to stand out as a united and disciplined body,' said the chairman.

We didn't get a word of what he said.

'From next week onwards, all students, boys and girls, are going to wear proper uniforms, provided by the college,' added the chairman.

'But why sir, how does it make any difference with what we wear? Who cares about an engineer's looks? His mind should be sharp,' said a boy.

The chairman came close to the boy.

'Just do as I say,' he glared at the boy, pointing a finger at him. And then, he left the class.

The boy felt offended. And, so did the others. After the lecture was over, the boy announced to the class, 'We are not bound by any uniforms. We shall not wear them.'

For the rest of the day, that was the topic of the discussion. Almost everyone agreed with the boy and decided not to wear the uniform. I however disagreed. The next day we were all sitting in the canteen.

'Hey. What is that?' Girish shouted as he saw someone.

A boy dragged a huge cart that was full of boxes. Everyone in the canteen rushed to the ground to see what the boy was up to. The boy stopped when the students crowded around him.

'What is all this?' Harsh asked.

The boy opened one box and showed the contents.

'Uniforms for us,' said the boy aloud so that everyone could hear it.

'A truck came and dropped the boxes outside the store behind the canteen. What do you say?'

The students looked at each other. Out of the corner of my eye, I saw Prakash. He stepped ahead and stood next to the boy. His standing there meant only one thing- Big trouble.

'I have an idea,' said Prakash.

I waited to hear what great or terrible idea was brewing up in his crafty mind.

'Someone get a can of petrol, please,' said Prakash and everybody looked at him, wide-eyed.

The boy who had brought the clothes fled the scene. Few minutes later, he came up to Prakash and handed him a can of petrol. Prakash kept the opened box on the ground.

'Please do the honours,' expressed the boy.

Everyone kept silent as Prakash fired his speech.

'South Africa. Mahatma Gandhi. Do you people remember what happened to Mahatma Gandhi and what he did there in protest? He brought forth the Indians there and told them to burn foreign clothes. Only a person himself or herself has the right to wear what one wants and no other. They want to impose a uniform on us and cage us. I am a free man. You all are free people. If we resist, we shall win. We shall burn these clothes,' declared Prakash.

'Please don't do it,' I shouted but no one listened. They all nodded.

'We don't take shit from anybody,' said Prakash and emptied the can of petrol by splashing it over the pile of clothes.

I watched in disbelief as Prakash lighted a matchstick and threw it on the pile. Everyone danced as the smoke rose. The smile on their faces ceased the moment a man stepped into the park. It was the principal. He slapped Prakash hard. Prakash said nothing but threw the empty can of petrol in the fire too and looked at the principal right in the eye. The principal didn't say anything but walked back to his office.

Since that moment, the entire first year batch went on strike. We always sat outside the college building. We did not attend studies even when our lecturers had come out of the college building to woo us back.

On the third day, we all hung around the canteen.

'That looks perfect,' said Prakash.

'Thank you,' said a girl who had painted 'No Uniform, Only Unity,' on a huge chart paper.

'Can I buy you a sandwich from the canteen?' she asked him, mesmerized.

'That would be really nice,' Prakash expressed and she dashed towards the canteen.

'The only girl in first year mechanical and she's all for him,' said Girish sadly as he also hailed from the machanical branch.

'There are so many girls in I.T., Computer and Electronics. Just go and talk to the one you like,' I encouraged Girish.

'Yeah, like it's that easy,' he said.

'Prakash, why don't we just go home? As such we are not attending the classes,' I said.

'We need to be visible at all times. At any moment, they may break down and negotiate,' said Prakash as the girl came back with the sandwich.

I was sick of Prakash's statements. What Prakash was doing was probably right. But it all had to end — pretty soon.

I left the canteen and advanced to the water cooler outside the mechanical workshop. After I quenched my thirst, I felt the movement of someone behind me. I looked behind and saw a young man looking at me gleefully. He was not a student, for sure.

'So here is where all you students come to drink water, huh?' he asked.

'Yes, but I am sorry I don't know you,' I said.

'I am so sorry. I did not introduce myself. My name is Vinay. I am the new Microwave Engineering professor in your college. I just joined yesterday,' he introduced himself.

I felt odd standing with the professor there.

'You look worried. Why?' he asked.

'Sir, if any student sees me with you, I'm dead. You are a professor,' I said.

'Calm down. I understand what you are going through.'

'You're not upset?'

'This happens in college. I led a lot of strikes in my college.'

Man, this guy was cool.

'Hey, just because I am a professor, doesn't mean I have devil's horns.'

'Sir,' I said.

'Please call me Vinay. I like it that way,' he said.

'Vinay, I don't like this strike, but I can't hurt my friends. What should I do?' I asked.

'Be with your friends. You people have to stay with each other for four years. You have to trust each other,' he said.

'Thanks a lot,' I said.

'Welcome.'

I rushed to the canteen and met Prakash.

'I got a message on my cell from a professor. He says the chairman is coming tomorrow to talk,' announced Prakash to all the first year students.

The next day at around 2 p.m., the college gates opened. A huge gleaming car entered and stopped in front of the main entrance. A number of men came out, including the chairman. They all walked through the main entrance and disappeared, while we all waited outside.

Half an hour later, a few professors came towards us. Vinay was also among them.

'Okay students. The chairman has come. Let's go inside,' said one of the professors.

'Will he agree to our terms?' asked Prakash.

'We'll see guys,' said Vinay.

We all went inside and sat in the auditorium. The door opened and the chairman stepped inside, alone.

'So, I see a gathering here, quite a display of unity among students - but for a wrong cause!' he boomed and everyone stared at him.

'We did nothing wrong. We will not be tied by uniforms in college. We are free here.

Discipline is judged by attitude, not by uniforms,' said Prakash.

'Come up here,' said the chairman.

Prakash hesitantly walked up to the podium where the chairman stood. The chairman extended his hand to Prakash, who was visibly startled.

'I believe in the uniform. But I cannot force any further. I give you what you call as your freedom,' said the chairman.

Prakash shook hands with him and all the students applauded.

A week later, I got a phone call in the morning. I woke up with a start when I heard the annoying noise. I picked up the phone.

'Please come to my place as fast as you can. And note down the address,' said the voice on the other end.

Who in the blazes is this? I wondered. I checked the number. *Aakriti* – was the name displayed on the screen. It was impossible.

'Aakriti?' I asked.

'Come to my home as fast as possible,' she said.

I couldn't believe it was her. Why did she want to call me?

'I have a class test,' I lied.

'You can skip it. Come fast,' she said.

'What if I say No?'

'I won't hear it,' she said.

'Fine, I am coming,' I said and hung up. I had to find out what she wanted.

I reached her home and she opened the front door of her luxurious bungalow.

'My parents are not at home. Let's go to my room,' she said.

We entered her room.

'Sit down,' she said softly.

Even in her pajamas, with her hair uncombed, she looked gorgeous.

She sat next to me. She was nervous. That was very unlike Aakriti.

'I broke up with my boyfriend,' she blurted out finally.

Why did she tell me?

'You must be wondering as to why I am telling this to you. It's obvious because I hurt you. But now I know one thing for sure,' said Aakriti.

That pregnant pause scared the shit out of me. My confused mind was further baffled by the flow of the following words.

'I love you.'

What followed suit seemed like a dream come true. Everything worked in slow motion. She closed her eyes and kissed me. She broke away to take a deep breath and said, 'Thank you for everything' before she started kissing again and I was too happy to bother about what she thanked me for.

I should have been bothered about that.

❑

THE SECOND SEMESTER

'Run!' I shouted at my partners-in-crime.

We had jumped over the college wall with the barbed wire fence and ran through the fields.

We had to reach the main road a kilometer away.

'Hurry up, you morons,' shouted Prakash.

'My feet are killing me,' screamed Harsh.

'Stop it right there!' boomed a voice from behind.

We turned around. On a motorbike, was a man who was speeding towards us.

'They sent a staff member after us on a bike?' Harsh shouted incredulously.

We ran at top speed as the biker chased us. We were at a good distance, so he could not see our faces clearly.

'Oh my God, look,' indicated Prakash.

Another biker along the field on the right was also chasing us.

'There!' I pointed at a biker who was riding in the field on the left.

'What did we do to deserve this? We are just bunking. They should let us go,' Harsh yelled as we hit the main road.

'We have defied the chairman, when he has come to visit the college. He won't stand it, nor would his henchmen,' I said.

That is what they clearly were. They were wearing no helmets. I could recognize them as the few people stationed in the college by the chairman whose only work was to kick students' asses.

'Someone help us.' I cried in despair. I feared being caught.

'An auto,' Prakash pointed as one suddenly appeared near the temple along the road.

In Haryana, an auto is not the usual tempo with a driver and a bench and a long seat at the back. This *Desi* contraption has a seat for the driver, two benches facing each other and another at the back. It faces outside. It is more like a Maruti van in the form of an auto-rickshaw. And so we hopped on the last bench and the auto throttled to life.

'*Bhaiya*, please drive at full speed. We are bunking and the college staff is chasing us,' pleaded Prakash.

The poor guy was supposed to fill in at least six people in his auto before he could go. But the young driver seemed to be excited at the very prospect of a chase and escaping the 'villains'.

'Okay, done,' he said and raced in top gear as we clung to the edge of our bench.

'They seem to be catching up,' Harsh said.

'No, they won't,' said a die-hard Prakash.

In spite of burning the gas at full speed, the bikers were not far behind. Suddenly, we came across the railway crossing, which made our college bus wait for ages if the gates got closed due to some oncoming train. Lo and behold, the gates started closing as a goods train was approaching. Our auto just managed to cross both the gates before they shut down fully. What a luck, as both the bikers got stranded on the other side of the railway tracks. We all heaved a great sigh of relief.

'So?' asked Harsh.

'Enjoy the freedom of true bunking,' said Prakash joyfully.

The bunking had been great. But a few days later, we heard of another thing.

The cultural fest was around the corner. There was the usual song and dance routine. However, there was one more option that I liked.

'Play?' asked Prakash.

'Yes,' I said.

'Have you ever acted before?' Harsh asked me.

'No. Never,' I declared.

'If you have never acted in a play before then how are you even suggesting such an idea?' exclaimed Prakash.

'Look. There are two simple reasons. A) It doesn't seem so hard and is easiest among all other options available. All this requires is crying, laughing and jumping — emotions, in short. How hard can that be?' I told them.

'And B?' asked Prakash.

'I really need to do something to impress Aakriti,' I said.

'Fine, but we do need girls,' expressed Prakash.

'We haven't even thought of a plot, a story, anything at all. How could you say that we need girls?' I asked him.

'He has a point,' said Harsh.

'Political plays, environmental awareness, social cause. None of them requires any girls,' I explained.

'Well, torn love stories, romance and spicy spoof of bollywood movies require girls,' said Prakash.

'We should think about it a bit,' I said.

'No. Everyone does a play that is political, social or intellectual. We'll just do a play that is sheer fun. Do you agree?' asked Prakash.

'OK,' I said.

'Anu would also play a part, obviously,' said Prakash.

Anu was Prakash's girlfriend – the girl in the mechanical section, who had painted the poster 'No Uniform, Only Unity,' during the strike in the first semester. After the strike got over in last semester, they became all lovey-dovey. It was sick.

'And who else?' Prakash said to himself.

I didn't want Prakash to think of more names.

'Anu has a pretty friend too,' emphasized Prakash.

Friend and pretty – these two magic words were enough to jam Harsh's mind.

'Say Harsh, what do you think?' Prakash probed Harsh.

'I agree with Prakash. To have Anu's friend would be fantastic,' beamed Harsh.

Later, I talked to Harsh.

'Anu is possessive about Harsh and a very strange character too, as far as I have heard. She shouldn't be with us. Her friend may turn out to be worse. And you agreed with Prakash,' I said.

'You don't know her friend or even been around Anu. Let's see what happens,' said Harsh. I didn't argue.

That evening, I went to see Aakriti at her home. Since the day Aakriti had first called me home and expressed her love, I had taken the liberty to visit her place, now and then.

'What are these?' I asked her, looking at a pile of notebooks lying helter-skelter, at the edge of a desk.

'Oh, those are my previous semester notebooks. I hardly open them,' said Aakriti and went out of the room.

I looked around. I saw an unlocked drawer in her desk. I opened it. It was a white envelope with the following words printed on it.

For Aakriti

The envelope was made of an A4 size paper and obviously it was a computer printout. That was strange. As I was about to open the flap, I heard the creek of the door. I turned, to face Aakriti.

'What are you looking for?' she asked.

'You,' I said and hugged her. She didn't ask further questions.

The next day and I and Girish were heading for the play rehearsals.

'She's beautiful. She's nice. Plus, she is fabulous at engineering drawing,' ranted Girish.

'You have it all wrong,' I said.

Girish was not participating for the stupid reason that he felt jealous and upset whenever he witnessed Prakash and Anu together. Anu was the girl we were talking about.

'What does Prakash have that I have not? What does she find in him?' Girish asked.

'Prakash is pretentious and deceiving. Didn't you see her at the strike? She was all for him. But she thought of him as a dominating figure. She likes men who treat others as slaves. So he had been lying through his teeth. He says that he drinks, smokes and also cheats to win, be it sports or academics. He says his friends appreciate him because they owe him a lot. And that we are his slaves. I hate Prakash for lying and the girl, who is happy with the lies,' I summed up.

We reached the empty classroom. Girish and I entered the room.

'Honey, wear this sweater,' Anu said to Prakash and hugged him tightly.

'This is Nishi,' said Prakash and introduced a beautiful girl who was sitting on a chair.

'Prakash, have you written the script and roles?' she asked.

'Yes,' said Prakash.

Prakash was the director of the play. He was also playing the lead role, the lover and Anu starred opposite to him. The story was that the boy and the girl loved each other. There was a twist however.

'The twist is that the boy is kidnapped by the villain and replaced by a look-alike. The look-alike has to appropriate the property of the family and is depicted here as a strong and charismatic character,' said Prakash.

The look-alike was also played by Prakash. The villain was Harsh and had to play Mogambo, the villain from bollywood movie *Mr. India*. His henchman was Gabbar, the villain from the famous bollywood movie *Sholay*. The role of Thakur was to be played by a friend of Girish. Thakur is also another character in the movie *Sholay*. Prakash explained that we had borrowed characters from different movies as our play was a spoof. Nishi hadn't been given any role as yet.

'The girl is suspicious about the boy whereas even her parents and those of the boy are not. The girl tells everything to uncle Thakur and he then assigns someone to find out the truth,' explained Prakash.

'Jai or Veeru?' asked Harsh, referring to *Sholay*.

'A beggar! It is another comic relief. He sits in the same position all day and gathers all the information through people passing by. Suhaas will play the role,' said Prakash.

The door swung open and everyone turned around. An old professor had entered the room and looked at all of us blankly.

'What are you students doing here?' he asked us.

'Sir, we are rehearsing for a play,' said Prakash and the professor flared.

'Get out or I will kick you all out.'

We all exited the room.

'Old Crackpot! I call it the Cross Room. I have marked it for myself,' said Prakash.

We got our University exam results a week after we had been kicked out of the classroom by the professor.

'Failed! I can't believe it,' as I looked at the F in my marksheet.

'Math,' said Prakash as he looked at the subject.

'I am done for,' I said.

I had impressed Aakriti with the math score in the internals. She loved it. And I had failed in it.

I went to meet Aakriti during lunch. I told her about my result.

'I hated that subject,' said Aakriti. I felt so relieved.

'But you said you loved it,' I said.

'I was lying. I was bad at it. That is why I pretended so that some wise guy wouldn't make fun of me. But you are equally bad and have failed in Math. I am proud of you,' she said.

I felt really happy. I had failed in a subject and my girlfriend was happy.

'But do try and pass in the reappear exam,' advised Aakriti.

'Yeah, I know,' I agreed.

In the next rehearsals, I got a chance to talk to Nishi.

'Nishi, tell me one little thing. I am sure you know about Disha. But you are sweet, nice and intelligent. How come you two are friends?' I asked.

'Tell me, why are you and Prakash friends?' she asked.

'We like each other's company. We understand each other,' I explained.

'Despite the fact that Prakash lied to Anu, so that she would become his girlfriend?' Nishi asked.

I looked agape.

'Prakash is smart, intelligent and innovative. But he also lied to Disha and always seeks attention. No one is perfect. It is a question of acceptance. You accepted his bad qualities and thus you are his friend. I also accepted the bad qualities of Anu. I know of Anu. She is highly possessive of anyone she loves and has strange priorities. So I am her friend. Simple.'

After the rehearsal, I talked to Harsh.

'I agree, Nishi is much better and smarter than Anu,' I said and Harsh smiled.

The unexpected happened in the rehearsals a few days later.

'Okay Gabbar, take a shot at me. Place an apple on my head,' said Prakash to Girish.

Harsh sat next to Nishi and talked to her. She still wasn't given any role.

I opened my bag to eat my lunch when an envelope fell out. I looked at the cover.

On the yellow envelope were printed the words 'For Aakriti.' I remembered it was the same envelope I had taken out of Aakriti's drawer. I had totally forgotten about it.

I opened the envelope and then read the letter. It was computer-typed, like the words on the envelope.

Aakriti,

'I like you very much as you know already. When last time I expressed my feelings, I really meant it. But what you think about me depends on you and I cannot change that. To show that I really care for you, I want to help you. I found out about your brother and am sending a cheque to help him out. Please accept it and my love.'

A bolt of lightning struck me. What the hell was this? Why was it sealed?

The letter was on a normal A4 size paper, typed in MS Word and was a printout. There was no date, no name, and no proof of the writer. It was in Times New Roman font and size 12. So, Mr. X could be anywhere. I was pitted against a faceless and nameless rival.

I was so immersed in the letter that I didn't hear Prakash's words. It was only when Anu shouted that I got to know.

'What are you doing? Listen to Prakash, you oaf,' she said.

'Please, I am busy,' I said, as I read the letter.

'Prakash did so much for you. You cling on to him and ask for his help. You are not even the dust beneath his shoes.'

That was it. She had crossed the limit.

'SHUT UP BITCH!' I shouted and everyone was stunned. I didn't look at Anu. I left the old library.

'What is this?' I asked Aakriti, as I met her in an empty classroom.

Aakriti took the envelope and read the cover. She opened it, saw the letter. She didn't read it, but kept it back inside.

'How did you find it?' she asked.

'It was in the drawer. I opened it. It was not locked.'

She suddenly embraced me and kissed me on the cheek.

'I understand you. I shouldn't have left it lying around for someone else to find out. It is something between us. After all, it is a letter from you,' she said.

I was speechless. I didn't see that coming.

'I don't know how to thank you. When you proposed me, I thought you were only infatuated by me. And a few days later, I got this letter. You found out about my brother and his addiction to drugs. It was a nightmare for me. I had spent sleepless nights either worrying about him or attending to him at the rehabilitation center. It was so bad. But, then your one cheque arrived and all my worries were gone,' she said.

She started crying. I didn't know what to do.

'The cheque…' I prompted and Aakriti spoke.

'I cashed it and found out the source account and the person who signed the cheque. He told me he had not written the letter. But someone had given him cash for the amount instead and told him to write a cheque in my name. He said that this person took the cheque and said that he liked the girl and had proposed to her a few days before. I remembered that you had proposed to me around that time. You really outdid yourself. I dumped my stupid boyfriend. You really care for me. I waited for a week near the bus stand and even mailed you. You did not reply even once. So I called you up in the morning.'

I remembered that during the strike period I hadn't read any mail, nor was I in any mood to meet Aakriti. That is when she must have mailed me.

'I love you,' she said and hugged me.

I met Harsh and Girish during the play rehearsals.

'So she thinks you are the envelope guy?' Harsh asked. He could not believe a single word I said.

'She got the letter a few days after I proposed to her. I have no idea how she got it and who gave it,' I said.

'It is really sad,' said Harsh.

'I don't deserve her. This guy does,' I said.

'What will you do now? Will you tell her the truth?' asked Girish.

'I don't know,' I said.

I looked at Prakash. He had not scolded me after I had shouted at Anu. He knew how crazy she was.

'How will you find out who the person is?' Harsh asked.

'The way fate put me in this situation, it will show me a way out,' I said.

One day Aakriti made me meet someone. Her name was Kavita and she was Aakriti's closest friend. Four days before the fest, we met her. Those days there were no classes and students were roaming around freely.

'Hi Kavita, do you know who this guy is?' Aakriti asked Kavita.

'Your boyfriend,' she said and both the girls laughed.

'Not just any boyfriend. He is the naughty one. He wrote that white letter with the cheque and helped my brother. My saviour,' said Aakriti.

'Wow,' said Kavita. She obviously knew the whole story.

'You guys talk to each other. I have to meet someone,' said Aakriti and parted.

'You are one generous guy. Aakriti is really lucky,' said Kavita.

'It was no big deal,' I played along.

Her expression changed in a flash. She looked at me aghast.

'You, Son of a Bitch!'

I didn't know how to respond to that.

'You are not the guy who called,' said Kavita in a low voice.

'Excuse me?' I said, trying to understand.

'You little insect, you are not the guy who called me that day. You are not the guy who mistook me for Aakriti. You are not the mysterious caller. You couldn't have written that last letter,' Kavita exploded.

'Yes, I haven't written the letter. I know that some other guy has written it. You have to tell me about him. Tell me what exactly did that guy say?' I asked.

'One night, an unknown number flashed on my phone and I picked it up. All I said was Hello, and some guy started speaking. He kept calling me Aakriti and said how much he loved her. He said he was the one who had been writing letters to her for a long time without mentioning his name or address. His voice was a bit muffled as I guess he had kept a handkerchief over the speaker to avoid recognition. He said that all he wanted was for her to love him as he was too scared to show his face. Then he hung up,' said Kavita.

'Didn't you tell Aakriti about this?' I asked.

'How could I? She would have been shocked. She never mentioned about any letter, so I guessed it was some other Aakriti. And well, she had received the letter because of which she thought of you as the writer,' said Kavita.

'But, how did she receive the last letter?' I asked.

'She found it in her hard bound project report,' revealed Kavita.

'So the guy is from our college,' I inferred.

'I know. But as Aakriti mistook you for him, she told me that she knew the writer. But he is still out there,' said Kavita.

'But you had his phone number,' I said.

'No, it was the number of some shop,' said Kavita.

'How did he sound, his accent?' I asked.

'His accent was *Haryanvi* and his English simply terrible,' unfolded Kavita.

'We need to find the previous letters. And if he is hiding his voice, then Aakriti probably knows him,' I said.

'Will he hurt her?' Kavita asked.

'I don't know. He just saved her brother,' I said.

In the evening that day, I went to Aakriti's house. Her parents were not there. Neither was she. As you must have guessed, I broke into her house. I knew a window that was generally open and broke into it.

I entered Aakriti's room and began searching for the letters. 'For Aakriti,' was mentioned on an envelope I found in an old notebook. It was similar to the previous one. I scanned through every old notebook and register and successfully found at least ten letters.

Actually, Aakriti's notebooks had a sort of a thin paper pocket inside. The sender had slipped letters in them. As soon as I got up, my cell phone rang. It showed Kavita. I stuffed all the letters into a small bag that I had and picked up the phone.

'Hello?' I asked.

'Aakriti met with an accident. I just got a call from her phone and some guy said that the owner of the phone has been taken to the AIIMS Hospital. Her car is a mess. Hurry up. I've been trying to call her parents, but their phones are switched off,' said Kavita.

My heart almost skipped a beat. At that very moment, I heard a car stop outside the house.

'Okay, I am reaching,' I said and rushed through the back door. I saw a lady standing outside the car. She was Aakriti's mom as Aakriti had once shown her photo. She entered the house and I sprinted to the main road. I took an auto. With my continuous shouting at the auto driver, it took me almost an hour. It was night time and it had started to rain.

I got out and ran as fast as I could. Kavita had told Aakriti's ward number and I jumped up the steps and dashed to save her life. I met the man who had called her using Aakriti's phone.

'How is she?' I asked him.

'Are you her relative?' he asked.

'I have to give my blood. Please call the doctor,' I pleaded.

'But it is done. Half an hour back, one boy came and willingly donated his blood. She is okay,' said the man.

I took a deep sigh of relief. Incredible, Aakriti was safe.

'But who was it?' I asked.

'Some tall, muscular and dark guy, who spoke in a Haryanvi accent,' said the man.

'Can you describe some more?' I asked the man.

'Well, I didn't take a picture of him. He wasn't good looking. He just came, asked me, rushed to give his blood and then left in such a hurry; I didn't get a second look. He said his name was Amar,' said the man.

'What is your name?' I asked the man.

'Shankar,' he replied.

'What happened to her?' I asked.

'I was crossing the road in the market when the accident occurred. I saw a car collide with her van at full speed. I took the girl to my car and brought her to the hospital. Her car is now with the police,' unfolded Shankar.

'Thanks a lot. I will inform her parents,' I said.

Shankar left and I sat beside Aakriti. The boy who had written the letters was not a stalker. He had saved Aakriti's life. My cell phone rang and I stepped outside the ward.

'How is she? Did you reach on time?' Kavita asked worried.

'She is okay. I couldn't reach on time. But, the boy who wrote the letter did. He gave her blood, half an hour back. He seems to fit your description. Plus, he is tall and well built,' I said.

'I finally was able to call Aakriti's parents. Their cell phone batteries were completly exhausted. I am sending a friend of mine to the hospital. You meet her and go back home, but please do not get caught by her parents. And, thank God for that boy,' said Kavita.

I agreed and waited for Kavita's friend. I looked at Aakriti's closed eyes. I was thankful to Kavita. Kavita's friend came and I left her in charge. I thanked the mysterious boy alias 'Amar' and went back home.

During the play rehearsals next day, I scanned through all the letters.

'Leave it,' said Harsh, 'he is not going to hurt her anyway. He just saved her life.'

'I don't care. I have to find out as soon as possible,' I told Harsh.

'Nishi and myself are going out to have dinner tonight,' Harsh announced.

'A date?' I asked him.

'If I told her that, she wouldn't have agreed. But please don't turn up,' requested Harsh.

'I won't,' I said happily and left the old library. I entered the computer lab on the second floor to take a printout. I sat on a computer and was about to begin when I heard a conversation.

'Come on Jaggu. Please type fast,' said somebody.

'I am typing fast. What were you guys doing? I thought you were the brainy ones,' said Jaggu, in his Haryanvi accent.

'You always make this spelling mistake. Express is E-X-P-R-E-S-S not E-X-P-R-E-S.

I don't know how you forget that extra S,' said the other person.

Express! I turned to face the computer. I scanned the screen.

The above Java program initiates the compiling of data. The construct is used to 'expres' the server. The function clearly 'sshows' the variables used...

I took out the letter I had found in Aakriti's drawer. It had the same spelling mistakes.

'Shut up Jai. This is an MS WORD document. It will correct itself,' said Jaggu.

'Not when you always turn the *editor* off. And please, even if this is not typed in Times New Roman, size 12, it won't make any difference. Forget the formatting,' said Jai.

It was all making sense. And it was terrifying too.

'What about the grand party you planned to give?' asked Jai.

'It can wait. I just bought a car so I will give you the party a month later,' said Jaggu.

'Let us finish this report anyway,' said Jai.

I slipped out of the lab without being seen by Jaggu or his friend. It was a terrifying and odd revelation. I could not believe it. But all the evidence was suggesting so.

The tall well-built guy, Haryanvi accent, same typing errors, and heavy expenditure recently— every jigsaw puzzle was fitting into the big picture.

'Where were you last evening?' asked Jai.

I turned around. Jai had just stepped out with Jaggu.

'Had some work. Urgent work,' answered Jaggu.

Jaggu and his friend entered another lab. I proceeded to go back for play rehearsals.

Jaggu was not even disclosing where he was. And, I had never actually concentrated on Jaggu's voice. I only remembered the sound of his punches.

A day before our play, Aakriti met me as she had recovered after the accident.

'How is my hero?' she asked me.

'Hero?' I asked. Now, what mistaken identity case had taken place?

'Oh come on. You saved my life. After I regained consciousness I saw Kavita's friend, followed by my parents. The doctor told that a boy named Amar had given blood for me. And of course, Kavita told me it was you. I knew it anyway,' she said.

'Is Jaggu in your classroom?' I asked her.

'What?' Aakriti asked distastefully as if she had eaten sour grapes.

'I was just wondering. I saw him in the computer lab doing some project report,' I said.

'Yes he is. But why should we care?' said Aakriti.

If Jaggu was in Aakriti's class, then it was really simple for him to slip a letter.

'Are you coming tomorrow to see our play?' I asked.

'Of course.'

'Bye then,' I said.

'Hey, I forgot to tell you one thing. Someone broke into our house on the day of my accident. My room was in a mess but nothing was stolen,' she said.

'Strange,' I said and said goodbye. I walked to the college ground.

'Hey you!' someone shouted.

I always avoided him. Yet, that day I wanted to talk to him – face to face.

'Where were you going?' Jaggu asked.

'To meet you,' I said.

His friends gathered around him.

'See the way he's talking to you. You should hit him,' said Jai.

'I will sure,' said Jaggu and raised his arm.

I was seething with anger, looking at Jaggu.

'This coward is dead today,' said Jaggu.

'You are the biggest damn coward in the whole world. You have no guts at all. You can't even tell a girl that you like her,' I yelled.

Jaggu was stupefied. His smile simply vanished and he suddenly stopped the swing of his arm mid day.

I was not just talking, rather spewing a non-stop volley of words:

The 7th Semester ——————————————— 43

'You think you can bully me. Bully your tongue – to let it tell the feelings to the girl you love. You gave her your blood. She is as such bonded to you. You don't need to write to her any letters anymore,' I said.

I detested Jaggu more than anyone. I looked at his panic-stricken face. It was confirmed. He was the mysterious writer.

'What, cat caught your tongue?' I asked him.

It sure did. I turned and walked away. I was walking out of the canteen after having lunch when Jaggu caught me.

'I have to talk to you, about Aakriti,' he said.

So he was a brave man, after all.

'Let us stand under those trees. I don't think you would like to be seen near me, chatting,' I said.

For the first time, Jaggu talked like a normal person, in a calm and soft voice.

'When I first saw Aakriti, I fell in love, instantly. I knew she was out of my league. In my second year, I started writing letters. I never dared to write my name. I didn't mind not receiving a single reply. But, I feared receiving a refusal. But, I am happy that she got all my letters,' Jaggu said.

'Not all,' I said and told him the whole truth.

'I sent her the letters. I even called her up once. How could she assume it was you? Did she never read any of those?' Jaggu asked anxiously.

'You called up her friend by mistake, not her. And she did not receive even a single letter. You hid them in some corner of her notebook. And, she hardly opened it ever. You never gave it to her properly. She only got the last one, because you had put it in the project report. And, she mistook you for me. That is it,' I said.

'Randeep,' uttered Jaggu.

'Who is he?' I asked.

'A guy who was supposed to inform me whether Aakriti read the letter or not. And, he always said she did.'

'But, you both are in the same classroom. That is how you must have placed the letters in her notebook. How did you not know that Randeep was lying?' I asked.

'You think I stayed in the class all day? Who was out their beating the other students? Me! My agenda of the day was to somehow slip the letter in one of Aakriti's notebooks and then leave the class. This Randeep guy is supposed to be a bookworm and stays in the class whole day. He was under my thumb. But, he betrayed me. I'll take care of him,' said Jaggu and took out a page.

I saw that it was the 'hit-list' of Jaggu, with a whole lot of names. Jaggu filled in Randeep's name as well.

'Are these the guys you plan to clobber?' I asked.

'Yeah,' he said.

'Leave it,' I said and snatched the paper from his hand and tore it into a hundred pieces.

'Hey, what was that for?' Jaggu shouted.

'This is how you have been ruining your career and love life. Forget these people, who have to be clobbered and stop writing on these pieces of paper,' I emphasized sternly.

'What should I do then?' he asked me.

'Forget the past. Come face to face with Aakriti. Tell her everything. The whole truth,' I said.

'But, if she gets mad at me then I am ruined,' stammered Jaggu.

'You do not have anything in control now. She hates you as she thinks you are a bully. Confess to her and let the fate decide,' I told him.

'So how should I meet her?' he said.

'You can meet her during the cultural fest. She is coming to watch my play. Sort it all out,' I said.

'Okay,' agreed a gratified Jaggu.

The next day was the judgment day for me, Aakriti and Jaggu. Also, of my play.

'Hi,' Aakriti said to me.

'Hi,' I greeted her.

'So, are you nervous?' she asked.

'No. Actually I wanted to talk to you about something,' I said.

'This is just like the way you proposed to me,' Aakriti laughed.

'I did not write that letter. I did not help your brother. I did not give you blood. I was not the one,' I said.

Aakriti was stunned. Her laughter had stopped.

'What are you talking about?' she asked in shock.

'I have someone here who wants to talk to you,' I said.

I turned around and saw Jaggu standing some distance away from me. Aakriti looked at him too.

'Jaggu?' she asked me.

'Yes,' I said and walked over to the stage. I met the rest of my group behind the stage.

'Are we all ready?' asked Prakash.

'Yes,' said everybody.

'Where is Anu?' Prakash asked.

'I got a call from her. She is ill today,' said Nishi.

'Who will play the heroine?' asked Harsh.

It was the correct decision. I thought so. I just said it

'Nishi! Though her role has not been assigned but she is well-versed with all the dialogues,' I said.

'Are you?' Prakash asked.

'Yes,' she said.

'My friend has not come today. There is no Thakur,' said Girish.

'Who will play the role of Thakur?' asked Prakash.

'I will,' I said.

'But you are the beggar. And Thakur instructs the beggar,' said Prakash.

'So what ? He instructs the beggar through a microphone in his ear. He disappears and the beggar arrives,' I said.

It was a crazy day - craziest ever. The other plays were good. Some even fantastic. In our play, we made a lot of mistakes. Nishi forgot some of her dialogues. Harsh forgot for a time that he was the villain. Gabbar, who was Girish, used the gun like a stick to beat the hero. A cast member shouted out that it was a gun. And when I was Thakur, I wanted to say something loudly. When Nishi brought me the mike to speak, I raised my hand to hold the mike. I forgot that Thakur had no hands. In all, people laughed at our silly mistakes in an as such twisted play.

The results were out. And the winner was announced.

'*Prakash and Group* for their excellent comedy and slapstick humour.'

I couldn't believe it. We were carried high in the air by students as true champions.

After the play, I met Aakriti. She was totally in tears.

'Thank you. I never knew what Jaggu really was,' said Aakriti.

'It's okay. Everything turned out to be fine,' I said.

Aakriti hugged me.

'May you be in true love with a wonderful girl,' she said.

Her own happiness was enough for me. I went to meet Prakash and Harsh who said they would be in the first vacant classroom on the ground floor.

As soon as I opened the door of the room, I heard loud voices.

'So, accept it,' Harsh said.

'I do,' said Prakash.

'What is it?' I asked.

'Close the door behind you,' said Prakash.

'What is it?' I asked him.

'I lied to Anu. I lied about you guys. I lied about myself. I demeaned you. I am the culprit,' said Prakash, looking down. Harsh and I stared at him.

'Then why didn't you tell me?' asked a voice.

We all turned our heads in the direction of the door.

Anu framed the doorway.

❑

THE THIRD SEMESTER

The moment we entered our third semester, or the second year, we felt jubilant. The Fresher Party was around the corner. And most important of all, the Mr. and Ms. Fresher contest. While professors wanted knowledge, we wanted to see pretty babes.

When the D-day arrived, the seniors promptly appeared in the college ground at a time when they were usually forced to by the professors. The girls had to do a catwalk and that too draped in a *saree*. The truth is that if you are hot enough, you will look good in a *saree* too.

But when she stepped on the ramp, all the eyes popped out of their sockets. She walked with such panache and elegance, with her hands tightened around the end of her blue *saree*, her cascading black hair caressing her fair skin and a cute 1000 watt smile that lit up her pretty face, such that every boy in the audience literally fainted.

'Hi, all you boys! My name is Simran. Nickname- Simmy,' she crooned on the mike.

The boys cheered and clapped at the fact that the girl was a real flirt. The professors looked unhappy with Simran's audacity. After her, some students came to perform a dance. I headed to the water cooler outside the mechanical workshop. When I quenched my thirst, Simran appeared beside me. She didn't drink water. She just stood there, looking preoccupied.

'Hey, is there a problem?' I asked.

She looked at me.

'I am so stressed,' she blurted and took out something from her purse.

'Are those some pills or something?' I asked.

'Not exactly, but they sure help.'

'Are you nervous for this fresher contest? Impossible, you were great,' I said.

'Oh come on. It was the biggest blunder of my life. I had never thought of it before I took part. I acted all natural and the professors were angry at me,' said Simran.

She was about to cry. I said what I could to keep her crying:

'Look. I'll tell you one thing. I don't know anything about you. But now that you have shown what you really are, you can't act all nice and coy. Let the professors accept you as you are. If you are naughty, be seductive, mischievous, whatever you want to be. All those who hate you can go to hell. That is Professor Suhaas's advice,' I said introducing myself.

'Thank you, Suhhas.'

'Good. Now do whatever dance or performance you have to present in the talent hunt,' I said.

She smiled and walked towards the stage.

I went back to my seat and sat with Harsh and Prakash.

'What took you such a long time?' asked Prakash.

'Nothing,' I said.

The second round started and it consisted of a 'rapid fire' round. It was Simran's turn.

'So shall we start?' asked the Compere.

'Yes,' said Simran.

'What is your favourite colour?'

'Blue.'

'What is your favourite dessert?'

'Chocolate.'

'One word that defines you?'

'Incredible.'

'What is your aim in life?'

'None.'

'Why? Everyone has an aim in life.'

In a competition if somebody asks you what your aim in life is, you frankly don't know.

But she should have said something.

'When I don't have any, why should I say I have?'

'Please elaborate further,' the compere prompted.

She took a deep breath and commenced.

'Like I said I have no aim in life. I may seem dumb and clueless for saying this, but I have a reason for saying so.'

Everyone looked at her with interest.

'A girl says that if she becomes Miss World she will help the poor and bring change. Once she becomes Miss World, instead of helping the poor she goes into acting. She could have still helped but she is too damn busy to help anyone. She might have truly aimed to help but her aim changed,' she further added.

I could see the audience was spellbound.

'I aimed to be a model. My parents forced me to become an engineer, so here I am. Tomorrow, people will say only MBA graduates get good jobs and this engineering alone is bullshit. If today you stand up proudly and announce that I am an engineer and will change the country then someone will laugh at you. He will tell you that millions of engineers pass out every year and many are still jobless. Then, you will ask the question to yourself. What is my aim in life?'

The question hung in mid-air and everybody seemed to be asking the same question.

'The truth is that there is never an aim in life. There are short term goals. Now if you ask my aim in life, it is to give me the courage to achieve whatever aim I have at the present and only let my own conscience decide whether my aim is right or wrong and not let it be decided by others.'

The moment she completed, the silence broke into a big applause.

After her, many girls came, did the ramp walk and did what they had to or say what they wanted to. But none of them had the edge that Simran had.

Finally, Mr. and Ms. Fresher pair was announced. I didn't hear who Mr. Fresher was. And, when Ms. Fresher was being announced by the compere, everyone sat on the edge of their seats.

'Simran,' announced the compeer and placed a crown on her head.

Everyone got up and clapped in unison.

When I went back to the water cooler, Simran appeared with the crown in her hand.

'Thanks a lot,' said Simran.

'Welcome,' I said and walked back towards my bus.

As I took my seat, I thought of Prakash. He was a charmer. He could easily talk to any girl. He could easily lie to anybody and get away with it. But he failed to lie to Anu. And, that landed him in a bitter break-up.

As you would remember about the last semester, after our play got over and we won (miraculously), I went to meet Harsh and Prakash. I found Prakash openly admitting that he had lied to Anu and also presented us to her in bad light.

'Then why didn't you tell me?' Anu had asked as we found her standing near the door.

'I love you,' blurted Prakash.

'You told me that you were popular, famous in school and you said that your friends praised you because you had helped them monetarily and otherwise. But you are a loser,' she said.

'You call a guy who loves his friends, helps them because he likes them and who doesn't smoke or drink, a loser? What kind of a girl are you?' I asked her.

'Practical. And thus, I like a practical and modern boyfriend. When Prakash led the strike I thought of him as a dominating personality who likes to keep everyone under his thumb. But, the fact is that he is too soft towards his friends and cannot conquer his enemies. He can never be my hero,' she addressed me.

'Then go and find a guy to your liking. Don't stand here,' I shouted at her.

'I sure will,' she said with finality.

With that, she banged the door and walked out on Prakash.

The next day after the fresher party, Prakash, Harsh and I were having lunch in the canteen.

'I have decided to party at my friend's room tomorrow night. In the boys' hostel,' said Prakash.

'No way! I am not coming,' I replied instantly.

'Think about it. I'll be back in a moment,' said Prakash and went to buy a juice.

'What's wrong with you?' Harsh asked me.

'How could you ever agree on this?'

'Prakash is going through a tough phase. Is it wrong if he wants to chill out with his friends?'

'I had to fight my way to the juice window. So, are you ready?' said Prakash on his return.

'Fine, but what is your plan?' I asked.

'We will stay at the boys' hostel tonight,' said Prakash.

'Then, what?'

'Neeraj, my friend, will buy the booze and fags. His friends will join us and we will have a gala time together. We will drink and talk through the night till we crash,' said Prakash.

'I thought you didn't drink,' I said.

'Well, I had a drink or two before. So, I was not totally lying to Anu. It's not bad.

I didn't like the idea at all — booze, hostellers, and bunking classes. But then, I observed Harsh's pleading expression and I agreed.

The party that happened the next night was crazy. Neeraj opened the bottles one by one and filled the glasses up to the brim. Two more of his friends joined us. One of them seemed a novice like me. The other discoursed on alcohol.

'The Russian Vodka is so good. I've never tried it. But one day I will,' he said.

Harsh and I and the novice just ate chips while Prakash and his friends emptied the glasses.

'Try some,' said Neeraj and poured some yellow liquid into my glass. I didn't even know who kept it there. I tried it. Bah! It was awful. I grimaced with disgust.

'Don't drink it neat,' said Prakash, pouring me some ice water and more liquid. I resisted, but Prakash made me drink forcibly.

'I hate it. Don't give it to me,' I said.

'Try this,' said Neeraj's alcoholic friend and filled my glass with a wee bit transparent liquid.

'Damn!' I shouted after I drank it. It burned my throat.

'That is Vodka. And you drank it neat,' he said and laughed.

'They don't like it Neeraj,' said Prakash.

'Fine, I'll give them some soft drink,' said Neeraj and took out a keg from the fridge.

He poured the soft drink in all our glasses.

I drank it.

'It's different,' I said. It sure was.

'Yeah, it is a new flavour,' said Neeraj as he emptied his glass.

Slowly, my eyes started to close. Before I passed out, I remembered only one thing that Prakash said that night.

'I hate you Anu, you horrible wretched girl.'

When I opened my eyes, the sun was burning my face as the sunlight streamed through the window. I clutched my splitting head. I just wanted to tear it apart. I looked around the room. Everyone was asleep. I checked the time. I gasped.

'Twelve Noon,' I said to myself. I got up to wear my shoes. But as my head pained, I sat on a chair and didn't move.

We reached in time for the 1:20 class. It was the class of my arch nemesis.

'Welcome, Mr. Suhaas! You are the most interesting student I have met till now. You failed in M1, got bad marks in M2 and now you skipped the morning class for M3. It seems like you want to spend some time alone with me. Or rather the principal,' said the math professor.

M is for math. M1, M2 and M3 are abbreviations for math in 1st semester, 2nd semester and 3rd semester, respectively. I had failed in M1 and not yet given the reappear exam.

To make matters worse, my hangover hadn't totally subsided..

'I am sorry sir. I will attend every lecture,' I said.

'That will be a great favour,' said the professor.

'Your friend got us drunk. And, you knew that,' I said to Prakash, as we sat in the canteen in the afternoon.

'I didn't. I seriously thought it was a soft drink.'

'You are lying. The same way you lied to Anu and hurt us.'

I really shouldn't have said that. Without uttering a word, Prakash left the canteen. He went ahead and sat under a tree in the college ground.

'You must be crazy,' said Harsh to me.

'I am not. Prakash was not in control yesterday. And his friends are not trustworthy as well,' I said.

'Well, Prakash didn't know that Neeraj had mixed some alcohol with the soft drink. In the morning, Neeraj apologized. When you passed out, Prakash said that he had done the wrong thing by being with Anu. But in his heart, he has feelings for her. So it is better that neither of us rake up her name again. Prakash needs to forget her, not be reminded of her. Stop giving him the guilt trip. Go say sorry to him,' said Harsh.

For the first time, I saw Harsh talk commandingly. And, I appreciated him for that.

He was right. I had crossed the line.

I walked over to Prakash and sat next to him. The shade of the tree was comforting.

'I am sorry. I just shot my mouth off,' I apologized.

'I made a bad choice. I liked her. She was cute, pretty. The best part was that she liked me, but for all the wrong reasons. And, I supported her reasons and pretended to be the guy she adored. I will never make the same mistake again.'

The third semester seemed tougher. It was the beginning of the second year, and the actual electronics and communication subjects became a part of the curriculum. Studying M1 was a big pain in the ass.

'Economics seems more interesting. It has nothing to do with our field, but is still one of our subjects. The professor teaches with such interest as if she knows the market by heart.

And, we can score higher marks to compensate with poor scores in other subjects,' said Harsh.

I agreed with Harsh. The economics professor enhanced upon the nuances of the market in such a manner that the students got involved with it. But, my problem-subject was of no interest to anybody.

'Look, none of us can actually help you in M1. You know how much we all have to deal with this semester. Either the math professor can help you, which seems pretty unlikely

or may be, a first year student,' said Prakash clearly.

A few days later:

'Neeraj says that he arranged some books and notes that could help in our assignments. But we have to stay tonight at the hostel. After all, we have only a few days to submit them and we won't be able to do it on our own,' said Prakash.

Copying was not a new thing for us.

'Nothing like that night will happen again,' promised Prakash.

So that evening, I, Harsh and Prakash stayed at the hostel for work. Girish stayed to give us company. We slogged it out from five to nine, hurriedly copying every word in the notes and books, same to same. At quarter to nine, I had finished my assignment.

'We are not done yet,' said Prakash and Harsh.

'Well I am done and going out for a walk,' I said and left the room.

I descended the steps and advanced to the gate. The guard was missing. I guess he went to have tea or something. I stepped out of the gate and looked at the sky. The moon was up and the sky was clear. I walked ahead. In the distance, there was the water fountain, ahead of which was the girls' hostel gate. I reached the canteen and grabbed some tea. There was no one around. I sat on a bench and sipped my tea in sheer tranquility. Suddenly, I saw this girl at a distance walking towards the canteen.

As she came nearer, I recognized who she was.

'Simran,' I called.

'Suhaas?'

'Yeah. Can I buy you some tea?' I offered.

'Sure,' she said.

We chatted a bit and then left the counter as soon as the canteen owner closed it for the night. A nice cool breeze started blowing as we reached the fountain.

'Goodnight then,' she said.

'Yeah,' I said and turned towards the boys' hostel gate.

'Wait,' said Simran.

'What?' I asked.

She didn't say anything for few seconds.

'I heard something,' she said.

'What did you hear?' I asked. Maybe she feared the dark. Or, maybe she heard the sound of an insect.

'It was some kind of rustling, in those bushes,' she said.

I looked around. The fountain was the point from where two different paths led to both the boys' and the girls' hostels. It was a sort of intersection of the paths of the two hostels. Along the path to the girls hostel was a garden that extended to the boundary wall of the college. On one side of the path, the garden was hidden by bushes. So, no one could see the garden beyond the bushes.

'It's nothing,' I said, but then I stopped in my tracks.

I heard a distinct rustling among the bushes.

'What is it?' Simran asked.

I slowly walked towards her.

'It might be a student. Or, some intruder,' I said.

'I am scared,' she said.

What could I say? I was scared too.

'Don't be. Here, I have a torch,' I said and took it out. I quickly pointed it to the ground and switched it on.

'Don't leave me,' said Simran. She stood close to me. I could hear her heavy breathing.

We heard the creak of a twig. We looked at the bushes. And, everything happened in a flash.

A thin, athletic, yellow eyed, four legged beast sprang from the bushes.

'AHHHHHHHHHHHHHHHHHHHHH!' Simran shrieked and grabbed me tightly.

Afraid, I pointed my torch at the creature. Its face was yellow with scores of spots all over its body. It turned around and leapt back into the bushes and disappeared. I was stunned and shocked. My senses became numb. I couldn't feel Simran gripping on to me, not letting me go as I looked at the spot where the creature stood. And then, I fainted.

I felt water touch my eyelids. I opened my eyes and saw a large number of students looking down at me. I looked around and saw that I was lying on the ground. I tried to get up and the lone professor helped me. I recognized him. He was Vinay, the professor with whom I had a talk during the college strike.

'Where, where is the leopard?' I asked.

'Relax. Just sit down and have some water,' said Vinay and gave me a glass.

'Calm down,' said Vinay.

His calm and peaceful manner made me relax.

'What happened exactly?' asked Vinay.

I told him everything that I remembered. Me and Simran heading back to the hostels, arrival of the leopard, my pointing the torch accidentally and finally fainting.

'At least you could talk,' said Vinay.

'Why? Where is Simran?' I asked.

'We all heard her shout and came running here. We found her in a state of shock and fear, crying. And, you were lying unconscious, beside her. She has not been able to talk coherently. Her friend took her back to her room. We will talk to her tomorrow morning,' explained Vinay.

I suddenly realized a great many people were staring at me.

'You should go back to the hostel too,' suggested Vinay.

'I'll take him,' said Prakash and held my hand. His timing was always perfect as he never missed a chance to be in the limelight.

'Let's go,' said Harsh and he joined Prakash. We cleared our way through the crowd and walked up to the hostel gate. Girish was waiting there.

'What happened?' he asked.

'Tomorrow,' I said and we entered the gate.

The next morning was a noisy affair. There were gossips galore. Few sickos had taken photos of Simran crying, with me lying unconscious the night before. It was pasted on the walls. Suddenly, I was a known face.

'Wow. Even I didn't get that much attention when I lead the strike,' Prakash said to me.

'How was it?' my classmate asked.

'Terrible,' I said to sum it up.

'Simran said today that she held tight onto you when the leopard came. Is that true?' said another.

'What? Is she awake?' I asked.

'Yeah. She woke up an hour ago,' said the classmate.

Just then, the door of the classroom opened. A professor peeked in.

'Who is Suhaas?' he asked. I raised my hand.

'Come with me,' said the professor.

All faces turned in my direction.

'Go,' said Prakash.

I left the classroom with the professor as several eyes followed me.

'What is it, sir?' I asked.

'It's about last night. The principal has called you,' he informed.

We finally stood before the principal's office.

'Go in,' said the professor.

It was the first time I had ever entered the principal's office. He had a neatly-trimmed moustache and sat on the other side of the desk. On the side facing me, a man sat in a chair.

'Suhaas, meet Kuldeep - the Forest Ranger. He is here to catch the leopard,' said the principal.

I shook hands with him.

'Suhaas. I would like you to tell me exactly what happened last night,' asked the principal.

I narrated him the entire adventure. The forest ranger sitting beside me also listened carefully.

'You said you were standing near the water fountain, right?' asked Kuldeep.

'Yes,' I said.

'Well, then it is simple. The leopard came for drinking the water from a nearby jungle,' said the ranger.

'Why would an animal come so far?' asked the principal.

'Forests are being depleted; ponds and lakes have dried up. The leopard traveled in search of water and found a way to cross the college wall. Thus, it discovered the fountain,' said the ranger.

'You think it might have come before?' asked the principal.

'Maybe,' said Kuldeep.

The principal looked gloomy.

'Can you take me to the exact place where you saw the animal?' asked Kuldeep.

'Sure,' I said.

I took him to the spot.

'What is behind those bushes?' asked Kuldeep.

'A garden.'

We walked into the garden and saw the boundary wall.

'Look at that tree. It is outside the college, but its branches extend inside the boundary. Any animal could have easily climbed it to come inside,' said Kuldeep.

He was correct about the tree, which was just outside the boundary wall.

'Let us discuss the plan with the principal,' he said.

The ranger was like a super sleuth who was not ready to tell what he had observed and deducted - quite like Sherlock Holmes.

We met the principal, again.

'I will need a volunteer to help me in trapping the leopard, tonight', said Kuldeep.

I wanted to get out of the room as fast as possible.

'And I believe this young man can be of great help as he has actually seen the animal,' said Kuldeep as he patted on my back.

I was trapped. There was no escape.

'Good. Then agreed?' asked the principal.

I nodded in agreement, as if I had any choice.

Suddenly, the office door swung open and Simran came in.

'Simran, are you feeling alright now?' asked the principal.

'Yes sir. I can attend my classes,' she said. Her eyes darted at me for a second, and then back at the principal.

'Fine, sir! Tonight, this young man will assist me in catching the leopard,' said Kuldeep.

Simran stood there and heard what Kuldeep had said.

'I should leave sir,' she said and left the room.

'Yes, and good luck to you boy,' said the principal and Kuldeep and I left the room.

Kuldeep and I fixed to meet at six when it would get dark, near the fountain. Kuldeep left and I walked along the hall.

I felt scared. What if the animal was not caught? What if I shouted or fell at the sight of it? As I turned left to enter another passage, I saw Simran leaning against the wall.

'So how are you? Why have you not gone to your class?' I asked.

'I was waiting for you,' she said.

'What for?' I wondered.

I did not know what made her do that. She was not frightened like the day before. But still, she hugged me.

'Simran?' I asked, unable to understand her gesture.

'Thank you so much. I didn't know who you were till yesterday. But you are a brave man. You held on to me when that leopard came,' she said.

I was glad she didn't think of me as a coward. And I was glad that she hugged me.

'I don't even know why you are willing to take such a risk,' she said.

I could not say that I had no choice.

'It's because I want to. I don't want you to be scared again,' I said.

I had not thought of it before saying it.

'Here,' she said and took out something from her pocket. It was a small locket. It was made of gold and had a sword designed on it.

'What do I do with it?' I asked.

'Wear it. It is for good luck. I wear it whenever I feel scared. But you need it more,' she said.

I felt the warmth of her skin as I took it from her hand. Good luck or not, I wanted to wear it.

'See you tomorrow,' she said and left.

Darn it! I had to help the ranger to capture the leopard.

I decided to stay in the hostel for the night. I was in Neeraj's room with Neeraj, Harsh, Prakash and Girish.

'You don't have to do this. Seriously,' said Harsh.

'That's what I say too,' said Girish.

'Is it really worth it?' asked Prakash.

'You sure man?' asked Neeraj.

My principal knew that I was supposed to capture the leopard. Kuldeep had insisted upon me. I could not go back on helping Kuldeep. But one thing worried me more. If Kuldeep would do the work alone and I had to face Simran, then I wondered the kind of conversation we would have.

Simran would say, 'I cried and sobbed for you for nothing! You didn't help the ranger to catch the leopard. You are no hero. Give my locket back.'

But I wouldn't give it back. It contained the warmth of her hand.

'Give it back,' she would say and snatch it away from me.

No, I wouldn't do that. I would never let that happen.

'I'll do it,' I said.

As soon as the minute needle struck six, I went to meet Kuldeep. I asked him the plan. He explained. We were to sit on the branches of the tall tree near the fountain. When we would see the leopard, Kuldeep would shoot a tranquilizer from his gun. The beast would become unconscious. Mission accomplished.

'Where will we sit on the branches?' I asked.

'There,' Kuldeep said and pointed towards the tree.

Kuldeep had created a strong wooden platform or *machaan,* used for hunting tigers from top of a tree, which we fixed on the branches. We climbed up the tree and sat atop the *machaan* to have a good view of the garden and the fountain from there. We sat with our legs folded.

'Good,' said Kuldeep.

Time passed slowly. It was killing me. As soon as the first hour passed, I could feel the tension.

'Relax. I am here to do the work. I just wanted someone to be with me, for the sake of company. It sucks being alone out here,' he said.

'I understand,' I said.

'The beast may show up in an hour,' said Kuldeep.

The leopard didn't show up. I knew it was getting with the evening melting into the night. I remembered that the leopard appeared around ten, last night. So, to pass the time, Kuldeep started narrating his life story as how he was a novice in the beginning, but now he had already spent eight years in the profession as a forest ranger. I checked my radium watch. It was only nine pm.

'I am an expert I tell you. But well there is a problem,' he said.

Problem? Hell, I didn't want him to have any problems. He was my shield.

'What sort?' I prompted.

'Well, my work is mostly surveying the forest, checking if everything was right. I mean, it is not everyday that I catch animals. I never do. I am an expert alright, no doubt. But I rarely do it. Lately, there have been complaints of lions attacking the few surviving deer. They are really hungry, you know. So, for a week I have been shooting tranquilizers. Thus, I am not really accustomed to keeping awake through the night. I feel sleepy,' he said.

Drat! What the hell was he blabbering about?

'But that problem is now solved. I have waking pills. Like people have sleeping pills to make them sleep when they can't, these work in reverse. They keep me awake. Better than coffee,' he smiled.

I didn't trust either his pills, or him.

'Well, we'd better be on a lookout,' he said.

More hours passed. What was up with this leopard?

'Kuldeep, you should take those pills,' I said to him.

'Yes, I should,' he said and checked his pockets. A lost expression set on his face.

'What?' I asked him. Kuldeep was making me angrier by the second.

'I lost them,' he said, checking all his pockets again.

'What will you do now?' I asked.

'No worry. I can remain awake. Just need some control on my sleep. I won't need pills,' he said and sat very alert.

I never remembered when I went to sleep. But when I woke up, I checked the time. It was three a.m. I was worried. Had the leopard come and left? Just then, my eyes fell on the tree outside the boundary and a chill ran down my spine. There it was- the ferocious nimble beast. It swiftly climbed the tree, jumped over the boundary in one long leap and advanced stealthily towards the bushes.

I looked to my right, at Kuldeep. The buffoon was asleep. And I thought he was on guard the whole time.

'Wake up,' I said to Kuldeep and I grabbed his collar and shook him, but he just didn't buzz.

The leopard has crossed the bushes and was heading for the fountain.

I took an extra wooden plank and hit Kuldeep with it. Still, he didn't move an inch.

'Get up,' I said and I stood upon the wooden *machaan*. That was a mistake. I suddenly slipped and fell through the branches.

'AAAAAAAAA' I shouted as I fell, but finally clung on to a branch. I looked at the leopard. The animal wasn't drinking the water but staring at me with his glowing eyes.

'WAIT,' I said. But the leopard rushed back to the bushes.

'STOP,' I shouted. Just as it was about to reach the bushes, it fell down on one side. I couldn't look up, but I knew one thing. Kuldeep was awake.

The next morning was fantastic. I really was the hero. And Kuldeep accepted that.

'When I heard your shout, I got up. I saw the leopard running to the bushes. That's when I fired the shot. You shouldn't have slipped though, it was clumsy,' he said.

Our photograph was to be published in some leading English daily.

'The principal was happy. The college staff was impressed. And the students crowded around the cage to see the leopard. After the leopard was taken out of the college premises, the students carried me all over the campus. It was like winning the World Cup. I could say it was the best day of that semester. When I reached the classroom, students gave me high fives and cheered. I embraced Prakash and Harsh.

'You did it,' they said.

'Yeah,' I said and kissed the locket.

Simran was standing just outside the classroom. We walked over to the college canteen.

'Where were you?' Simran asked.

'Busy,' I said, as if people had been following me all day long. Actually, they did.

'Congrats. You did it. Now, you have become popular,' she said.

'Yes.'

'You were there with me, when I was scared. Is there any way I can help you?' she asked.

I should have asked more. I should have told her to hug me one more time. But, what I asked was equally important.

'Teach me math,' I said.

'That's it? Nothing more?' she asked.

'Not for now. You are a first semester student and M1 is one of your subjects. No one in my batch would help me and I hardly know any junior. I would be grateful,' I said.

'Okay. Done,' she said and smiled.

'Here, thanks for your locket,' I said, giving it back to her.

'No. Keep it,' she said.

'Why?'

'You never know when you might need it.'

Prakash and gang seemed keen to celebrate my success, which in fiscal terms meant I was paying for the party. So on a weekend, we decided to go to view a movie, followed by lunch. We went to PVR Priya in Vasant Vihar. As I spent over Rs. 100 per ticket, we got good seats in the second last row.

'Here they are,' I said as we checked our tickets to sit down.

'Can you sit on my right?' asked Harsh as we chose our own plush seats.

Just for a moment, I looked at the last row. My glance fell at the corner two seats.

I was shaken by what I saw. Maybe, there was something wrong with my vision. Or, may be, it was true.

I sat back in my seat.

'What happened?' asked Harsh.

'Nothing,' I said and the movie began.

On Monday, I went back to my boring schedule. Still, I made some new friends

Many students wanted to be my friends. And then, the fourth period was the math class.

My arch-enemy entered the room and ridiculed me as usual. I hadn't done anything wrong. But I did not reply back. As soon as the period ended, I got up from my seat. The math professor came near me.

'Wait till the other students leave,' he said.

I clenched my teeth and controlled my anger. I waited, till all students left for lunch, one by one. The professor and I were alone.

'You know, your marks are going to dip drastically,' said the professor.

'Why?' I asked. There was no emotion in my voice. I didn't show anger, surprise or anxiety.

'You are not paying any attention. You don't listen in the class. You failed in M1. You are bound to fail in M3,' he said.

'I am trying my best, but if you continue giving me less and less internal marks every time then how will I get good grades?' I asked.

'You accidentally caught a leopard. Big deal! So, now you roam around the college with your chest out and mind full of false pride. How dare you talk back to me like that?' he asked.

I felt like replying back sarcastically. But, only one word came to my mind.

'Economics,' I said.

As I expected, the colour of his face got completely drained.

'Economics,' I repeated and he fell back in his chair.

'What?' he said as if he had no inkling. But he knew exactly what I was talking about.

'Saturday. PVR Priya Cinema. Corner seats. You and the Economics professor, together, hand in hand. I saw it all. I was in the row ahead of you,' I said.

'So? How does that affect me? Will you tell it to the principal? No one would believe you.'

'I won't tell the principal. I will simply tell your wife, who teaches in this college,' I said.

'What do you want?' he pleaded.

'Here is the deal. My internal marks better be good this time. Great, I mean. You shall not censure me in front of the class. And, you are genuinely going to help me pass M1. If you agree to that, then I will forget what I witnessed,' I said.

He placed his hand on his chin as if he was thinking it out.

'Do you agree or not?'

'Agreed,' he said with a resigned tone. I left the class and he sat there, clutching his head.

I felt bad for the Economics professor. She was a nice lady. I had even talked to her a few times. She obviously didn't know the idiot had a wife. And the poor wife didn't know what her husband was up to. I couldn't actually reveal that as it would ruin the wife's life and my career too. I knew that it was really bad that a student like me was interfering with personal matters of the staff, but she had to know it, someday. I had to wait for that day. After all, people never know what designs the destiny holds for them.

❏

THE FOURTH SEMESTER

'Did you clear the math paper?' asked Prakash.

'Yes, Simran helped me,' I said.

'Of course she did, after the leopard saga.'

'No, she was simply keen to help me.'

'Whatever you say,' said Prakash.

After Aakriti, I couldn't think of any other girlfriend. What existed between me and Simran was merely friendship.

'There is a project competition for second to fourth year students,' said Harsh.

'So?' I asked. I knew Harsh's answer. I was ready with mine.

'We can make one,' said Harsh.

'I applaud your confidence, but we can't do it,' said Prakash.

I was glad that Prakash agreed with me at one thing.

'How?' asked Harsh.

'First of all, we are second year students. We have hardly any knowledge of subjects like embedded systems, microcontrollers or sensors that would help make a good project. We just can't do it,' he said.

'Besides, you know how we pass our practical exams. We mug up the readings, make chits or smuggle in our lab files to write the readings,' I said.

'We know the fourth year students will win since they know the theory and take help from their professors,' said Prakash.

'Someone might help us too,' said Harsh.

'That would be really good, if possible,' I said.

I did not want to give false hopes to Harsh, but l was still keen to provide him a glimpse of the light at the end of the dark tunnel, especially after the episode with Nishi.

'See you later guys, I have to break the news to Simran,' I said and left.

Nishi, as you would remember, was Anu's friend. During the rehearsals of our play, Harsh had spent a lot of time with her and liked her, but it seemed like a one-way street. Harsh met her to talk about Anu's break-up. But, Nishi said she had a fight with Anu and broke the friendship.

'But that doesn't mean I don't like you,' said Nishi to Harsh.

The duo dated through the second semester. But then, he got the bad news of Nishi getting admission in a much better college, which she had been trying for. Finally, she had to leave.

In the third semester, Harsh and Nishi communicated through phone and SMS. But at the end of the third semester, Harsh tried to call Nishi but in vain as the number did not exist any more. And, he never received a single call or message from her. So, Harsh was keen to take part in the project as it would take his mind off Nishi for a few days.

I stood outside the mechanical workshop on the ground floor and saw Simran busily sawing a wooden block. I waved to her and she came outside and told me to meet her in the sixth period. Sixth being her free period, we met in the old library where no one came.

'So?' she asked.

'I have some good news,' I said.

'You passed?' she asked.

'Yes. But not just passing marks. Look,' I said and showed her the DMC.

'Wow. How did you impress your professor?' she asked.

I didn't want to tell her about the deal between me and the professor.

'So I guess we should party?' she asked.

'Where will your friends come?'

'I mean just the two of us. Is that wrong?'

I felt something amiss.

'Won't it look odd?' I asked.

Simran laughed.

'When I being a girl don't feel odd, why should you? Just two friends together,' she said.

'When and where then?' I asked.

'Saturday evening, DT City Center,' she said and I agreed.

Saturday was a week away. I had to wait and watch.

The next day was full of sunshine. The technical fest was only a month away.

After the third lecture, I slipped out of the lab to drink water. I met Vinay.

'Good morning,' he said.

Vinay was the Microwave Engineering professor whom I met during the strike

'Good morning. Vinay,' I said.

'I heard there is a technical fest next month and some project competition also. Are you participating?' he asked.

'No. I am in the second year, and no subject of use in any project has been taught as yet.'

'I might be able to help you.'

'Really?'

'Yes. But you got to cooperate.'

'Sure. Whatever you say.'

'You will have to make primary efforts like searching for projects related to microcontrollers, microprocessors,' he said.

The microcontrollers and microprocessors were not even taught to us then.

'Can't you tell us about one of your own projects?' I requested.

'Suhaas, do something by yourself.'

'OK, when should I meet you?'

'Next Monday.'

'Thank you, sir,' I said and shook hands with him as if we had agreed on a multi-million dollar deal.

When I told the news to Harsh, he was ecstatic. Prakash was still skeptical. I hated that.

'Wow, that would be great,' Harsh said. He was happy to use his grey matter for something creative to get his mind off Nishi.

'I still don't want to take part, I don't trust the capability of the professor,' said Prakash.

'He obviously knows more than us. He will be of a great help,' said Harsh.

'I and Harsh are going to search for a list of projects on the Internet. If you are ready to come then we'll go to the Computer Lab on the first floor,' I said.

Prakash, with no choice left, came with us. We typed 'microcontroller', 'microprocessor' and 'sensor' and got a huge list of projects. We narrowed it down to twenty projects.

On Saturday, I wore the most fashionable clothes I could find.

'You look fantastic,' said Simran when we met in the evening. We watched a movie and roamed around the mall.

When we ordered Pizza, we had time to talk before we could eat.

'It's been a great day, hasn't it?' she said.

'Yeah,' I said.

'I have to tell you something.'

'We can talk after we eat the Pizza.'

'It is much more important than your Pizza.'

What catastrophe hit you? I wanted to ask.

'Why do you think I wanted to come with you, alone? Just for some party, for math?

It was only an excuse,' she unfolded.

My brain got clouded with endless thoughts.

She placed her hand on mine. I looked at it.

'I like you,' she said.

Aakriti had proposed the same way and I had still not been able to cope with the outcome.

'I have to go.'

'What?'

'I'll meet you tomorrow,' I said and got up from my chair to leave.

'Did you even hear me?'

'I am really sorry Simran. But I have to go,' I said.

'I have never been rejected by a boy. That is because boys are after me. But I don't mind even if you don't believe me. Or don't like me for some reason. The reason is, I like you,' she said.

She was a year younger and sought by many other boys. Why did she like me?

'Why do you like me?' I asked her.

She gave the same baffled expression again.

'Look Simran. You are great. You helped me and there is no doubt you are the second prettiest girl I have seen, no offence. But if you have any knowledge of my past, I can't risk it,' I clarified.

Her expression changed. From confused, she became sad.

'I know what you mean. But I too have my reasons. You were there with me when the leopard attacked. When I said I was scared, you said 'Don't be.' No one ever told me not to be scared. I know you caught the leopard for me. Admit it. You feel something for me too.'

'I need time to think,' I said and got up.

I took out my wallet and placed some notes on the table.

'For the bill,' I said.

'You are cruel,' said Prakash on Monday.

We were sitting in the empty microwave lab, waiting for Vinay.

'Don't lose her. If she really likes you,' said Harsh.

'Hello guys, ready huh?' said Vinay as he entered the lab. He came with a stack of books in his hands at a quick pace.

Harsh looked at him fondly. Prakash was not impressed. He yawned.

'Suhaas, you told them what to do?' asked Vinay.

'Yes, we narrowed down to twenty projects. You can tell us what we can work on,' I said.

'These five,' pointed Vinay.

'You mean to say that we are incapable of doing any others?' said Prakash.

'Sir, I saw the other projects. They also look good. Can we not make them?' asked Harsh.

'Look guys. The projects I have select are of two types. The first are those that have been often repeated. Others are those that require complex code that you cannot obviously write,' said Vinay.

Vinay's statements made a lot of sense to me. And Harsh nodded with me. Prakash was visibly furious.

'Guys, I have given you the five names. Choose amongst them. And I assure you, we will be able to make a reasonably good project,' said Vinay.

We left the lab and headed for our classroom.

'We won't be able to win this competition,' said Prakash.

Harsh and I said nothing.

That week was a hectic one. Our assignments and surprise tests did not seem to cease.

'Okay, what else do we have to do?' I asked Harsh as we got out of a lecture on Thursday.

'We have NM and Fundamentals of Management assignments left,' said Prakash.

'Fundamentals of Management' subject was taught by the same lady professor who taught Economics in the last semester. And, our math teacher was teaching NM. I had never told Prakash and Harsh about the affair between the two.

'What does the NM professor's wife teach?' I asked Harsh.

'His wife left the college. She used to teach English to the first year students, but she resigned,' said Harsh.

'Why?'

'Don't know. She was a nice lady.'

'Whoa. You know her?' I asked.

'Yes. She used to teach in my section in the first semester. When Prakash and you were in a different section,' said Harsh.

'Come on, we have to rush to the Digital Electronic lab,' said Prakash and we paced our steps.

As we entered the passage to the lab, we saw a woman standing outside the lab.

She was talking to the D.E. lab assistant.

'That's the NM professor's wife,' said Harsh.

She was an attractive person. Tall, slim with an erect posture.

'Mam,' Harsh intervened in the dialogue between the two.

'Hello Harsh. How are you?' asked the wife and talked to him. I didn't know why the math professor cheated on her.

'Okay. I have to go,' she said.

I entered the lab with one last look at the math professor's wife.

'Okay. Now we have lab work too. How will we concentrate on the project to choose?' Prakash asked me before the last lecture.

'That means you believe in Vinay?' I asked in return. I wanted a straight answer.

'I admit it. He is focused. We cannot do it alone,' said Prakash.

I was happy that he was with me. Harsh was already on my side.

I was fed up of all the work piled on us. So I decided to bunk the last lecture to finish the assignments.

It was winter time and the air in the college building was freezing. In hope of warmth and a ray of sunshine, I stepped into the balcony on the second floor. I heard someone crying. It sounded like a woman. I opened a classroom door, and a woman turned to look at me. It was the math professor's wife.

'I am sorry. I came in by mistake,' I said.

'You shouldn't be sorry. He should have been for doing this to me,' she said and cried again.

She was really upset.

'I mean, what did I do wrong? I played the perfect wife,' she continued.

I tried to calm her down.

'Madam, I know all about it.'

'How do you? You are a student, right?' she asked.

It was a good sign. Conversation at least made her stop shedding tears again.

'I am his student. He was teaching math to me since the first semester. In the third semester, I went to watch a movie in a cinema hall, when I saw both of them,' I said.

'The Economics professor is innocent. A month back, my husband went to the college and I was ill so I had stayed home. He forgot his cell phone and I saw a message. It had a woman's name and she sent a love message. I found out that it was the cell number of our economics professor. I met her and she revealed that she didn't know that he was already married.'

She took a deep breath. She needed it.

'I knew it was my husband's fault. I waited for three weeks for him to confess. I wanted to hear the truth from him. But he didn't say it. So a week before, I told him that I knew the truth. I told him that I would quit the job and divorce him. I came today to see him for the last time,' she said.

Her crying had stopped. She looked outside the window.

'What you are doing is wrong,' I said to her.

'I don't think so,' she said.

'Just think about it. You are leaving the job you love. You are leaving the man you love, even without giving him a chance to repent and sort out his ways,' I said.

She looked at me. She listened to me intently.

'I'd say I hate him more than any professor I have ever met. My reasons are logical. But your reasons for hating him are illogical. I know he lied to you, but you do not know the real reason. If anyone has to quit the job, it is him. Not you. If you leave him now, you will never know what he has to say. You had a reason to love him. You should also have a reason to hate,' I said.

I thought of Aakriti. I and she had broken up because of a reason.

'What is your name?'

'Suhaas,' I said and left the room.

'So, this is the best,' said Vinay on Friday as we narrowed down to the project we intended to do.

'An electronic walking stick for a blind man,' I said.

'Yes,' said Vinay.

'Here is the description I downloaded from the Internet,' said Harsh.

'It warns a blind man of the dangers around him. The stick warns us in case of a fire or if you are stepping into water,' explained Vinay.

'Wow. That is good. Something to aid the blind people,' I said ecstatically.

'This is not an original project. I mean, not only has it been done in foreign countries, other colleges have done it too. If it is available on the Net, it might be in a shop,' said Prakash.

'Wow, a great way to encourage us,' Harsh said sarcastically.

'Prakash is correct. Someone else might have done it too. But no one has made this in our college. It also matters as to how much does the student learn and improve upon it,' said Vinay.

'Fine,' I said to him.

'Then let me tell you some basics,' said Vinay and opened his notebook.

He gave a brief structure of the project.

'Sensors,' said Vinay and explained about them.

'Thermometer is a sensor that senses our body temperature.'

'Our sensors will show change in heat, light intensity with change in resistance,' he said and got on to explain more. He gave a brief idea of microprocessors, their types and moved on to the microcontrollers.

'Take these books. Here is a book on microcontrollers. This one is on sensors and transducers. I'll quickly mark the pages you need to read,' he said.

'He is superb,' exclaimed Prakash.

I hated to visit the college on Saturday. It was an off day, but I had to get some books from the library. During lunch, I saw Simran heading to the canteen.

I ran to the canteen.

'Do I know you?' she asked me as if I was a stalker.

'Yeah, you know me. I am your boyfriend,' I summed up.

'I'm so happy,' she said and hugged me tightly like on the night of the leopard incident.

On Monday, when my dear friends came, I told them about Simran.

'You did it! Good,' said Prakash.

'You are back in love my friend,' said Harsh.

It was an important day. Vinay had told us that on Monday, all the fourth year students who would be participating would be displaying their projects.

'Wow,' we said as we entered the lab full of projects.

Many groups of students were around us.

'We won't be able to see such a display until our fourth year,' said Harsh.

'True. Even if most of these projects are crap, they all look beautiful. And these students, all look real engineers,' said Prakash.

I felt something sharp and slithery rise up my sleeve. I looked at my arm and shrieked in shock. It was a caterpillar.

'Get this off,' I said and Harsh brushed it off my sleeve.

'Relax guys. It's a robot,' said a boy who came forward. He had a remote in his hand and wore glasses.

'Who are you and what the hell is this?' I gasped.

The boy picked up the 'caterpillar' and pressed a button. The caterpillar climbed up his sleeve. It looked at us with its glassy eyes.

'My name is Deven. This is my project. A remote controlled wireless caterpillar. It took us hell of an effort to make it wireless controlled,' said the boy and patted the caterpillar which in return, made a noise.

'What are these colours and the changing shades?' I asked.

'Oh, we spray-painted on the steel,' explained Deven.

I had run out of adjectives to describe that thing. It was beautiful, almost real.

Deven turned to us.

'So, what are you guys making?' he asked.

We had no answer.

The next day, the atmosphere in Vinay's lab was of extreme tension. Actually, only we were tensed, Vinay was not.

'Can we even match that? No,' said Prakash, describing the caterpillar.

'Our project should be something like that,' said Harsh.

'I agree,' I asked Vinay.

'It's amphibiotic robot – a robot in the shape of a reptile, like a serpent, frog or caterpillar. Deven's caterpillar turns into a serpent too,' said Vinay.

'But it is great. Let's make it,' said Harsh.

'You can't. It's not that easy. Deven is one of the most brilliant and hardworking students in electronics. He spent months on this.

You are blinded by its beauty and accuracy, but you will not be able to make this as your own project,' said Vinay.

I was at Harsh's home. After college got over, Prakash and Girish went back to their homes.

'Wow, these guys look mean,' I said, looking at the posters on his wall.

'That is the front man. The other guy is the bassist. That is the drummer,' Harsh explained.

Metallica, A.C. D.C., Children of Bodom, the names kept rolling off Harsh's tongue and didn't end. The only rock or metal or whatever bands I had ever heard of were Rolling Stones, Deep Purple, Beatles and Pink Floyd.

'I listen more specifically to metal that is within rock. There is Nu metal, Death metal and many more genres,' he said.

'I don't know. This rock music sounds more like noise pollution to me,' I said.

'Some like it. Others don't. Those who like it are loyal to it,' he said.

It was another side of Harsh. I always saw his outer self - serious, concerned and hardworking, like an angel. But this was his inner world.

'This is so much relief. I don't think about Nishi,' he said.

It had been a long time since Harsh had mentioned Nishi. I guess that music was a balm to his heartache.

We sat in Vinay's lab during the last lecture on Thursday.

'Did you study the circuit diagram?' asked Vinay.

'We had a look at it,' said Harsh.

'Well, keep it with you,' said Vinay as he took out a bag from the cupboard. He turned it upside down and emptied the contents on the table. A board with holes, wires and tiny objects came out.

'What are these?' I asked.

'I bought these for you people. You will make five sensors and then connect them to ports of the microcontrollers and provide output to the buzzer that will vibrate according to the desired sensor,' said Vinay.

'So how do we go about it?' asked Prakash.

'You will make the entire circuit yourself.'

'What? No way. We might do it wrong,' said Prakash.

'I've never made a circuit before,' I said.

'Don't be afraid of making mistakes, that's how you will learn. Look at the circuit diagram and make it accordingly. I will help you,' he said.

He pointed out at each component and told what they were. We designed a few sensors and placed a microcontroller on the printed circuit board.

'We can do the rest later,' said Vinay.

That day we made some progress. It took more time to understand than to solder on the board.

On Saturday too, we went to college.

'On Monday, your professors will select what projects to be displayed in the competition,' said Vinay.

After I went home, I called Simran.

'Are you coming to see my project?' I asked.

'I am not going to the college next week. There will be just the preliminary rounds for every competition for the fest,' she said.

'But won't you be taking part in something?'

'No, I get bored. I will come next Tuesday to see your final project. I am sure you will qualify on Monday,' she said.

'Hope so.'

'Good luck.'

'Thanks,' I said.

The crowd on Monday was unbelievable. The preliminary rounds for quizzes, puzzles and other activities were taking place, including the project competition. The decision panel had three professors as judges. Each group demonstrated its project to the panel.

'What is this?' a judge asked the first group.

'Our project sir,' said a boy in the group, surprised by the question.

'It is only a small circuit. Where is the power supply? What about the coding?'

'We have to finalize those issues,' said the boy.

'Well, finalize them for the next year. Sorry. Next project,' said the judge.

Me, Prakash and Harsh exchanged glances. There were so many questions and statements they posed to the groups. A few of them were like:

'Is it economical?'

'How did you exactly fabricate that circuit? Explain step by step.'

'Do you even know what you are designing? It's not a robot, just a scanner.'

'Please, in the name of god, don't take part in this competition.'

I was scared by that one. Our project was part complete. What if it was rejected outright?

'Magic Wand by Prakash and group,' said the panel.

As we came forward, the panel looked at our project intensely. It was a tall stick with the circuit fitted. We had not completed it. But we knew our concepts well.

'Okay please tell,' said a judge.

We had decided that Harsh would speak first, followed by Prakash. I was least confident in explaining.

'Its name is Magic Wand as it is no less than magic for a blind man. It senses fire, obstacles, presence of water, informs as it falls and also detects light,' said Harsh.

He went on to explain the whole thing. The judges were quite impressed.

'Your project is not fully functional. But your concept and presentation is good,' said a judge.

I was happy.

'Next,' they said and continued further.

The last project was presented by Disha, the geek goddess. Almost everyone hated her as she was a bookworm and didn't mix with others. But, she was the brightest.

'This is an anti-theft environment. This box detects motion of any object through sensors and sounds an alarm.'

Her project seemed fantastic. Sure enough, it was selected. But the panel said only one other project was selected.

'Magic Wand. That's it folks,' declared the panel.

Our group was overjoyed. Out of the seven projects presented by our class, we were among the two selected.

'Great,' said Vinay, when we told him the news. He met us after lunch. I tried contacting Simran. She wasn't picking her cell.

'She must be sleeping,' said Prakash.

I was about to agree when we passed outside a class. The door was open and students were busy participating in a written quiz.

'It is the prelims,' said Harsh.

I wasn't listening to him. I was staring at the girl on the first bench.

'Simran,' I said.

'What?' asked Harsh.

'Look,' I said and pointed to the girl. Harsh and Prakash looked at her.

'Yes, she sure is Simran,' said Prakash.

'Why did she lie to me about not coming to college? Is she avoiding me?' I asked both.

'Chill out. She must have changed her mind at the last minute,' said Harsh.

I didn't know the truth. But I hated any girl who lied.

'Yes,' said Vinay on Wednesday. We had completed the circuit, done half the wiring and fitted the voice processor too. I recorded my voice for each sensor. The voice processor was a 'record' and 'play' device. Harsh pressed on the button and I shouted in the miniscule mike 'Beware, Fire!'

'Excellent. Now if there is a rise in temperature near the fire sensor, the processor will play 'Beware, Fire!' The sensor array, the microcontroller and voice processor will be connected. Project complete,' said Vinay.

We were glad. But we had three days left in the week to complete it with the final touch ups. It would be good to go.

'Should we take it home?' Harsh asked.

'Keep it in the Head of Department's office. Only professors and other staff members go there. It won't be affected. My lab assistant took the keys for the cupboards in this lab,' said Vinay.

I woke up next morning with the ringing of my cell phone. It was Prakash.

'Listen Suhaas, the 'Magic Wand' is broken. When we went to the H.O.D.'s office yesterday, I kept it at one corner of a sofa. But this morning we discovered that some fool sat on it and the wires were all broken, along with the circuit board. Even the voice processor was not working. It's a lost case.'

'What the hell are you blabbering?' I shouted.

'I doubt that Vinay can repair this,'

'So, are we out?'

'No. I have a solution. Meet us at this place that I am telling you.'

I noted the address and we all met there. And, Prakash proposed his plan.

'You want to buy a project?' I yelled at him.

'We have no other choice. The stick is way beyond repair. And I don't want to lose,' said Prakash.

'I don't believe it. Where is the stick?' I asked them.

'We couldn't bring it. But I took some pictures of it,' said Prakash.

Prakash took out his cell phone and unlocked it. He then showed me various pictures of our broken Magic Wand from different angles.

'It's a mess,' I said.

'See? I know a shop here where we might get a better project,' said Prakash.

'Harsh, do you agree?' I asked.

'I don't see a way out,' said Harsh.

I reluctantly agreed. Prakash entered the 'project shop' he knew and Harsh and I stood outside. An hour later, he came out.

'It is done. Tomorrow evening, we get the new improved project,' declared Prakash.

I had never felt so guilty before. The Friday morning looked the foggiest and the darkest.

Prakash was relaxed at the fact that we were getting a readymade project. And as per his decision, Harsh and I were to stay home till Monday. I walked to my couch. I was just about to sit when I received a call on my cell phone. I didn't know the number, but I picked it up.

'Suhaas, I am Vinay speaking. I want you, Prakash and Harsh to come to the college right away.'

In two hours, all three of us were standing in front of him.

'Prakash, it seems a brilliant plan! You wanted to buy a new improved project. No drudgery, no use of hands. Winning is important. Effort or knowledge is not,' said Vinay.

Vinay tried hard to keep his cool.

'How did you know about it?' asked Prakash.

'I got a call on my phone and I overheard the conversation between you and a shopkeeper. You had accidentally called me as your phone was probably unlocked,' said Vinay.

'I must have kept the book I had on the phone,' said Prakash.

'After I hung up, I checked for the project. And I found this,' said Vinay and opened his cupboard. He showed the broken project. The circuit board was broken and the wires were in a mess. It looked more horrible than the pictures Prakash had shown me.

'I need to talk to Suhaas, alone,' said Vinay.

'But sir…' Harsh started but Prakash interjected.

'Come on Harsh. Let's go outside,' said Prakash and they left the lab.

Vinay stood near the window, silently.

'Did you ever think why was I willing to help you all?' Vinay asked me.

I shook my head.

Vinay spoke. And when he did, I didn't interject.

'When I was a student, just like you, all I had some theoretical knowledge. I mugged up everything. During my last year in college, I met a professor who taught me how to turn the theory into practice. I didn't top my college, but I surely knew lot more than any other student. I did M.TECH from another okay college and submitted my research papers for college and continued writing even during my PhD. Currently, I am at par with the top engineering professors in this country and abroad.'

I was stunned by his introduction.

'I have no fancy degrees to boast about. But I am still here, teaching at the same post as your other professors. Why? The reason is because I tried. I stand here before you, as a proof that an underachiever can succeed and not just survive. I look at every student and see a powerhouse of capability. Millions of engineers pass out every year, in spite of getting admission in lousy colleges. But they do nothing to become true engineers. If they are in a bad situation, they do not try to fix it. You need to rise up from the ashes, not fall back into them.'

I just stood there, listening to every word Vinay said. I could feel his rage, his anger that I had seen for the first time.

'For me, your success is my success. And my late professor's success,' said Vinay.

I felt disgusted for agreeing with Prakash.

'Suhaas, I had trusted you. I feel ashamed of not you, but myself,' said Vinay.

Just then, the door of the lab opened. Prakash ran and fell on Vinay's feet.

'I am sorry. But please, don't blame Suhaas or Harsh. It was entirely my decision. We have no time,' said Prakash.

'Get up!' said Vinay, 'I have seen projects in worse conditions. Now, we will fix it,' he said.

Vinay was a magician. He almost fixed it.

'By Monday, it will be fully functional,' said Vinay.

'So, it was not impossible to repair it,' I said after we left the lab.

'Yes. And please, enough of the guilt trip,' said Prakash.

'Let us check out what those third and fourth year chaps are doing,' said Harsh.

We went to the lab and the projects seemed much more completed. Students were busy assembling and tuning in their projects. I could see Deven happy with the caterpillar on his left arm. Another group made a flying helicopter with a spy camera on top of it. The helicopter's legs extended as it landed on the ground.

'Wow. It is a third year project. Good,' said Harsh.

One group had nothing but a circuit board and legs to show. If anyone asked them what they were doing, their leader Mathur spoke.

'This is a small circuit of what we are making. Our project shall be the best and you all will know what it is on Tuesday,' he said.

Pure arrogance, I thought.

'We have finally done it,' said Vinay on Monday evening.

The stick was detecting everything. It was great.

'Tomorrow is show time. Be ready and best of luck,' said Vinay to us.

The D-day had arrived. I called Simran, hoping she would wish me good luck. But she didn't pick up. I went to college.

'Here it is,' Harsh said, showing the stick in a case.

There were four judges, two hailed from the industrial sector, one was the professor of a reputed college and there was one very senior professor.

'Guys, did you check everything?' asked Vinay.

'Yes,' said Harsh.

The senior professor walked towards us. He stood next to Vinay.

'Excuse me, do you remember me?' he asked Vinay.

'Not really, sir,' Vinay replied.

'Come on. We met last year in the Goa conference. I saw your presentation on superconductivity and MRAMs. I gave you my card also. But, you never called,' he said.

'I am sorry. I had been rather busy,' said Vinay.

The judges left us after a few minutes to check the project of the first group. We had brought a torch, matchbox, water bottle as sources of light, heat and water. I switched on the torch and the light fell on the photo sensor. The LED started blinking, but the voice processor did not say anything.

'It's not working ,' I informed Prakash.

'Damn it. Try for the fire sensor.'

I lit up a matchstick and placed it in front of the fire sensor.

'Light! Light!' cried the voice processor.

'This is bad,' said Harsh.

'It can be fixed if we call Vinay,' said Harsh.

Harsh called Vinay, but no one picked up the phone.

'Let's try ourselves,' said Prakash.

For two hours, we fiddled with the project. In that period of time, the judges had seen four projects. Amongst them was Disha's project. For some reason, it didn't work and judges were not happy.

'There is a one hour break. I request all the groups to rejoin after that,' announced the organizer.

The judges left the lab. We rushed to meet Vinay.

'After it was broken, the connections became lose despite our efforts. Let's try again,' said Vinay.

An hour was enough to fix it completely. It was working fine.

We went back to the lab and saw that the rest of the students were already present. The judges were looking at Deven's caterpillar project. The senior professor was amused when the caterpillar ran up his sleeve. They advanced next to the dinosaur robot next to me. Finally, it was our turn.

'Okay, please explain your project,' said the senior professor to us.

Harsh explained it in great detail with confidence.

'Demonstrate,' said the senior professor.

We lit up the matchstick and the voice processor screamed 'fire'. We kept the stick in front of the wall and it warned for obstacle. Everything worked perfectly.

'Not bad for a group of second year students,' said the senior professor.

'We did it,' Prakash said to me and Harsh.

The judges saw the helicopter project. They were impressed by the use of the spy cam.

The last project was of Mathur and his group. He had named the project 'Multiple' and he took it out of a wooden box. It was miraculous.

It was a helicopter with legs so that it could stand. Two arms protruded from windows. And then the helicopter walked! It looked like an android that walked with hands at its sides. The hands and legs moved efficiently.

'It is a weapon of the future,' said Mathur.

An hour later, the results were announced. The helicopter with spy cam came first. Deven's caterpillar was second. And Mathur's 'multiple' came third.

'I checked the list. Our project came in fourth. So, we officially do not get a prize,' Harsh said.

'The idiot,' said Deven as he stood near us.

'Congratulations,' I said to him.

'Mathur bought that project. The cheat,' cursed Deven and walked away.

I, Prakash and Harsh went to Vinay and told him everything.

'We cannot do anything about it. But you guys did well. I saw from the outside,' said Vinay.

'Yeah. We didn't get anything. But at least we learnt,' I said.

'Let's go back to the lab. Just for the heck of it,' said Vinay.

When we entered the lab, there was a lot of whispering going on.

'Is something wrong?' Vinay asked us.

Just then, a boy standing near the judges announced:

'The judges want the 'Multiple' group to demonstrate the project again. The project did not work. The group could not figure out what the problem was. The judges believe that the project is not entirely the work of the students. It has been disqualified. The new positions are as follows. The caterpillar is first. The spy helicopter is second and the third is Magic Wand. Congrats.'

We leaped with joy.

After I reached home, I checked my e-mail. Simran had sent a zip folder with some pictures. I opened the folder. It contained pictures of Simran with another boy. Hugging and holding hands. I remembered the boy. He was the one sitting next to Simran in the written quiz preliminary round. Was it a joke? There was another possibility. She had sent the folder by mistake.

The next day, I waited outside the auditorium where the final round of quiz was being held. I had found out that she was in it too. She had lied to me about not going to the fest.

After the quiz was over, the audience came out. Simran stepped out with the first prize trophy. I mixed with the crowd and followed her. She and her friends entered an empty classroom and I stood outside and listened to their conversation.

'How is your boyfriend?' they asked Simran.

I waited to hear my name. I wanted her to say 'Suhaas.'

'Kunal is okay. We took a few pictures of ourselves together with his cell phone. They are cute. Priya, I sent them to you. Did you check your mail?' Simran asked her friend.

'Not yet. I will,' said Priya.

So that explained it. She had mailed the folder to the wrong address.

'Why did you lie to that leopard boy Suhaas that you liked him?' asked Priya.

I pressed my ear harder against the door.

'After Suhaas had caught the leopard, he became famous. Even he doesn't have any idea of it. I could tell that from his face. No pride, no arrogance. But then everyone associated him with me. I got attention more than when I became Ms. Fresher. I proposed to him so that he would show his affection and everyone believed that we were a couple. If you girls want any work done by any junior, just tell that Simran knows Suhaas. He is, after all, their hero,' boasted Simran.

The bitch! I fell for her, the heartless beauty queen.

'Good, you lied about not going to the fest. He would have totally ruined your fun time with Kunal,' said Priya.

'I have to drink water. I will come back in a moment,' said Simran.

Simran stepped outside.

'How is Kunal?' I asked her.

She jumped. Before she could say anything, I said what I had to.

'Your friend Priya did not receive the pictures, I did.'

She looked at me agape.

'Your fake boyfriend is not a toy. Go seek attention for what you really are.'

'I can explain,' she started crying.

'Oh, by the way, I had to give you something,' I said.

'What?'

'This,' I said and threw the locket she had given me.

'No. Please let me explain,' she pleaded, but I had turned in the opposite direction. I didn't bother to look back. My chapter with her was over.

I sat in the grass and breathed under the shade of trees. It was the last day of the fest and two days after my break-up with Simran. Just as I looked at the college building, the math professor's wife stepped out. She walked towards the college ground.

'Hello,' said the math professor and sat next to me.

'Sir, what are you doing here?'

'You saved my marriage. You gave me a second chance. And you are asking what I am doing here? I have come to thank you,' he said.

The truth dawned upon me. So, his wife did have a talk with him.

'She is not leaving her job. And, now we are back together as one loving family. You are a bad student, but a great human being. I won't be teaching you anymore. But if I did, I'd give you a perfect score. Just for the attitude,' he said and got up.

'She should not have mentioned my name to you,' I said.

'She had to say it. Otherwise, I would have kept wondering who gave her the idea to resolve it and show me the right path.'

He walked towards his wife and they embraced each other, I felt that everyone deserved love. I assured myself with one thing. Someone better was waiting for me, hopefully.

❏

THE FIFTH SEMESTER

'It feels good to be called a third year student,' said Prakash.

'From next semester, companies will start coming. We have to think about our jobs. And nothing is going to be simple,' contemplated Harsh.

It was our first day in college after the holidays. We were heading for the canteen before the first lecture when we heard the shout of a boy.

'Stop it! Leave my arm! You are killing me.'

'Who is that?' I asked.

'Maybe I know who it is,' said Harsh.

As soon as we entered, I saw what I hadn't seen in two years. A boy was writhing with pain. His arm was twisted and held behind his back, by a girl.

'Chew your words, before I eat you alive,' said the tomboy.

She was different. She had her ears, nose and eyebrows pierced with rings. Her hair were boycut and she wore torn jeans and a black sweat shirt.

The crowd in the canteen watched the girl, the boy and his friend with utmost interest. But they all kept their distance.

'I'll take care of her,' walked in another boy, rolling up his sleeves.

'Just remember one thing. You asked for it,' said the girl.

The next five minutes were literally from an action movie. The boy with the folded sleeves had directed his fist towards the girl when she punched him in the face with her empty hand. The boy fell against the food counter. The girl threw the boy in pain towards the juice counter.

'She broke my leg,' said one of the casualties.

The crowd looked on as the beaten boys moved out of the canteen.

'Let's buy a juice. I don't want to be near her,' said Harsh to me.

My eyes were fixed on the girl. She took a cigarette box, a sandwich and left the canteen.

'Who is she?' I asked in amazement.

'Trisha,' said Harsh.

'You know her?' asked Prakash.

'She is in the same year and department as us. Only, she is in the other section. As you both remember, in the first semester, I was in the other section. I knew her. Everyone knows that she's a total bully,' said Harsh.

'Okay, let's go to attend our first lecture,' I said.

'Now you all are third year students. You better be more focused on your studies,' said the Microprocessor professor.

I didn't need to be alert for the microprocessor lecture. After what Vinay had explained about microprocessors for our project, I wasn't much worried about the subject. I just leaned on my seat when someone whispered in my ear.

'I do agree. It's going to be a boring lecture.'

I looked behind to see who it was.

'You are Trisha,' I said as I recognized her.

'And you are Suhaas.'

While the lecturer taught us, I conversed with Trisha without looking back.

'Why did you beat up that guy?'

'He abused me when I was buying a fruit juice.'

After the lecture, I met Harsh.

'She's not so bad. I had a talk with her,' I told him.

'Stay away from her.'

'How can you say that?'

'She picks up fights like we change our clothes.'

'Harsh, let's bunk tomorrow,' I said.

'No. Didn't you hear what the microprocessor professor told about the training?' asked Harsh.

I hadn't heard a word of what the microprocessor professor said.

'A fortnight later, each of us has to give the presentation,' said Harsh.

After the fourth semester, all the students were required to undergo training in a company during the summer holidays. And then, they had to give a presentation on it.

'We will have to prepare for it,' said Harsh.

Harsh was really a good student and he got training in a company. I had a reference so I went for training, though attending just for two days as I was assured of the certificate. Prakash didn't get any training, so he tried frantically for a fake certificate.

'I don't want to think about the presentation right now,' I said.

After the lecture, we were supposed to have three hours of discussion on presentation. The discussion was held in an empty classroom and a professor was lecturing us. After half an hour, I quietly slipped out of the room when the professor turned his back. I found Prakash at the water cooler.

'Are you bunking?' I asked.

'I am going to meet a hot chick from second year.'

'Best of luck,' I said and Prakash left.

I went to the college ground and rested under a tree. A few minutes later, Trisha walked up to me with a sandwich in her hand.

'Can I sit next to you?' she asked.

'Sure,' I said.

We talked on and on. I felt free, relaxed and at peace with her. I released all the pent up tension inside me by telling her everything about my past love life.

'Why does every relationship end up like this?'

'It was not your mistake. You proposed to Aakriti and expressed your feelings. What happened later was not your mistake.'

'And, Simran?' I asked.

'You were not aware of her intentions,' she said.

I couldn't imagine Prakash or Harsh discussing about my past love. She told me about herself. She mostly hung out with boys like an equal. She was outspoken and powerful. She said she never tried to impress boys.

'A boy proposed to me, when I was in Class Tenth. He was from my locality,' Trisha said.

'So, what happened?'

'He cheated me. I went to a McDonalds near my home and found the rascal with another girl, two tables away,' Trisha said.

'Did you slap him?' I said.

'I should have. But, that was not the point. Something fine and delicate broke within me as he broke my trust,' Trisha completed.

To hear about things like love and boyfriends from a girl like Trisha was like listening to Beethoven talking about motorbikes instead of music.

'We should go back. The presentation session will end soon,' I said.

'You go, I am better out here.'

When I reached the room, I took a peep inside. The professor was not there. I slipped inside and sat on the last bench. Harsh came and sat next to me.

'Prakash is also not here. Were you both together?' he asked.

I didn't want to mention Trisha, lest he got angry.

'Yes. I came back, but he's in the canteen.'

'You are lucky, the professor gave us a ten minute break and left the room,' said Harsh.

When the professor came back, I had the cheek to ask him a question.

'Sir, everything else I understood. Except for the last points you told.'

'I would tell you gladly. You have been an attentive student,' said the professor.

I ignored the stares of other students, including Harsh.

'Wanna bunk today?' asked Trisha on the first day of the presentation.

'No, I want to see every presentation as I am scared about mine,' I said.

'I won't turn up before my presentation,' announced Trisha.

'Sit next to me,' I said.

'Why do you want to be with me? I am a scary bully who beats people up.'

'C'mon, I know you better. Just don't bunk for my sake,' I said.

'Okay, fine. I'll listen to my music then,' she responded quietly.

I liked her company, but didn't have the guts to tell her. So, I was happy when she sat with me when some dude gave a presentation. The presentation was supposed to be given on MS PowerPoint. The computer was connected to a projector that displayed the PowerPoint slides on a white screen hung on the wall. So in actuality, the presenter looked at the white screen instead of the computer monitor. The PowerPoint slides on the computer were changed by another student, called a helper.

The duration for the presentation session was for two hours in which four people gave their presentations. I looked at Trisha next to me. She had fallen asleep.

'Thank you for sitting with me,' I told her at the end of the presentation session.

'I slept. I got bored.'

'It doesn't matter. I just wanted you to be with me.'

'Did you do anything about your own presentation?' asked Harsh, a few days later.

'First is your presentation, then Prakash and the last is mine. I'll prepare,' I said.

'Have you even read the material you got from the training?'

'Don't worry about it. You should help Prakash.'

'Forget about him, I am more concerned about you.'

We were in the third week of our presentation. Every week we had two days of presentation- Tuesday and Thursday. My class fellow Dharm's presentation was the last on Thursday.

'So, that would be the end of it,' said Dharm, wrapping up his presentation.

'I finished my pending assignment,' said Trisha, who sat with me.

After the first day of presentation when Trisha sat with me, she never bunked a single presentation. For some reason, she sat next to me during the entire session.

'Please show me the last slide.'

Everyone looked at the new professor who asked this question. He sat there for no particular reason, during Dharm's presentation. The usual professor looked at this new professor.

'Sure sir,' said Dharm and the helper displayed the last slide.

'This diagram is incorrect,' said the new professor, who was from the CSE Department. He was not even supposed to be there. But, somehow no one objected to that. Not even our professor who sat next to him.

Dharm looked at the diagram.

'It is correct sir,' he said.

'You are explaining a block diagram about a particular Internet connection structure. I am an expert at that.'

'I do not doubt that sir. But I did my training sincerely.'

'Show me the second last slide.'

The helper changed the slide.

'This is absolutely wrong,' said the professor.

'Sir, everyone knows it is correct,' said Dharm.

'Maybe a few hundred years ago, not today,' said the professor.

That made Dharm angry. As such he was a short-tempered guy.

'Sir, it is correct. Please ask me a valid question,' said Dharm

'Fine! Then tell me, did you actually go for the training?'

'Yes sir.'

'I don't think so.'

I knew that Dharm was right. And that the professor was barking up the wrong tree.

And then, all hell broke loose.

'I don't think you are a professor then,' quipped Dharm.

'So that is how you talk to a professor, huh? '

'Sure. I am not scared,' Dharm said rolling up his sleeves.

At that point, the students in the first row got up to stop him. Our own professor got up.

'Please gentleman,' said our professor.

'I think you need some treatment,' said the CSE professor.

'Bring it on,' said Dharm.

Everybody got up. They all surrounded the two.

'Please. He's just a kid,' said our professor to the C.S.E. professor.

But, the C.S.E. professor and Dharm looked at each other in the eye.

'Go Dharm, go,' shouted Trisha beside me.

A few heads turned in my direction and I told Trisha to keep quiet. But there was so much commotion that Trisha's voice could have barely reached Dharm's ears. Some students were urging them to fight, most of them told both parties to stop quarreling. In a few minutes, the quarrel moved outside the presentation room and flowed out into the main hall.

'Go back to your classes,' shouted the professor over the din to the students. I and Trisha left with the others. The argument between the two was still going on when I walked out with Trisha.

'What's wrong with you Trisha? You were encouraging Dharm to hit a professor,' I said.

'The professor was nasty.'

'Dharm can be suspended for talking like that.'

'Better than losing his respect,' she said.

Trisha was crazy. Or maybe her opinions were different.

Next Monday, I had a talk with Harsh.

'Where is Prakash?' Harsh asked.

'I don't know.'

'Well, you are too damn busy to talk to Trisha. You don't have time for anybody,' Harsh said.

'How has Trisha anything to do with Prakash? Prakash goes wherever he wants, how am I to keep a track of him?' I asked.

'He's dating someone,' Harsh inferred.

'Yes he is. Her name is Sapana,' I said.

'Sure. By the way, I heard Trisha motivating Dharm to fight. She might motivate you also someday,' said Harsh.

I ignored it.

'I am going to drink water and will meet you in the lab,' I said and went to the water cooler. Harsh didn't argue and left for the lab.

'How are you Suhaas?' asked Anu as she appeared beside the water cooler.

'Fine.'

'I have to talk to you.'

'Why?'

'I can't get Prakash out of my mind. All day and night, I think about him. I am never at peace,' she said as she followed me.

'Why are you telling me this? You didn't break my heart,' I said.

She stood in front of me and blocked my path.

'All the while I liked him because of his sweet lies. I forgot how he made me feel special. After him, I met boys who actually were the way I had thought Prakash to be. But none of them made me feel wanted or special the way Prakash did. I really missed him,' said Anu.

'Forget about Prakash. Do you even keep track of Nishi? She was after all your friend. Tell me.'

Anu was speechless.

'Harsh and Nishi liked each other. If you were really her friend, today they would be together. When you cannot remain faithful to your friend, how can you remain faithful to anyone?'

Anu really had no answer.

'You need to sort things out, Anu. First think about your friend and then Prakash. Maybe you feel guilty and not love Prakash. Think about it and then talk to Prakash.'

Anu nodded and descended the steps to go to the ground floor. I looked at my watch. She had taken a lot of time. I hurried along to the lab.

I entered the Electronic Simulation Lab and discovered Trisha working alone on a computer. I sat beside her

'What are we doing right now?' I asked her, as I looked at the computer screen.

'Who was that girl you were talking to at the water cooler?'

'Did you hear our whole conversation?'

'I couldn't stay all day long to hear you two.'

She kept working on the program and didn't look at me.

'How does it matter? She is just some girl,' I said.

'Well you never mentioned this 'just some girl' to me. '

Trisha was jealous.

'She is not my friend. She was Prakash's girlfriend,' I said.

Trisha turned to look at me in a flash such that I almost fell from my chair.

'Are you lying?'

'No,' I said.

She heaved a sigh of relief.

'So why did she talk to you?' asked Trisha in a normal way.

I told her about the whole conversation with Anu.

'Horrible girl,' said Trisha.

'You were angry at me a few minutes ago. You have to make up for that.'

'How?'

'I am unable to write any of these programs. It is your responsibility to make me pass in the external practical,' I said.

'Done,' she said, with a 'thumbs up' sign.

On Thursday, Harsh gave his presentation with alacrity and confidence.

'Okay, slow down boy,' said the professor, alarmed at Harsh's speed of explanation.

'That was the last slide. Thank you,' said Harsh.

'You did excellent work,' I said.

'Have you seen Prakash? He missed today's presentation session also.'

'Must be dating or bunking. Hey Harsh, can you help me with my presentation?'

'No.'

'What? I thought you were ready to help.'

'I was, but that is history. Now you do it on your own. I have some pending work.'

We went back to the classroom and found Prakash.

'Where have you been Prakash? You have skipped every presentation,' stated Harsh.

'I got a fake certificate. I know all about the presentation. I am collecting material.'

'How will you do that, by dating?' asked Harsh.

Prakash looked at me. I looked the other way.

'Well, for your information, yes. She's a great girl. I talked to her today. She helped me to get that certificate. Now she will find some material.'

'You are using a girl for getting material for presentation? That is sick,' said Harsh.

'Are you mad? No. We get well and are happy together. She is in second year and offered to help ,' said Prakash.

'So you will give the presentation on Thursday, right?' asked Harsh.

'Absolutely,' replied Prakash.

'I can help you,' said Trisha, the next day.

'Really. That would be great,' I said.

'I will be able to help in editing the content you received by the company,' she said.

'When will you help me?' I asked.

'Not this week. From Monday onwards,' she said.

On Sunday, I got on to the task of extracting my data. I searched for the manuals that the company had given me. I had to explain something that sounded cool.

'NCA, Next Computer Architecture,' said Trisha on Tuesday.

We had come out of the presentation session and Trisha explained to me.

'Focus on that. Rest is junk.'

On Thursday, my mind was focused on Prakash. So was Harsh's. Every passing minute leading to his presentation was painful. Finally, his name was announced.

'Prakash,' called out the professor.

Prakash stood up and walked over to the professor.

'Sir, I will give my presentation later,' he said.

I was shocked. Harsh's mouth fell open.

"Have you not completed your presentation?"

'I have, sir. I can show it to you right now, at this very instant. But it is not perfect,' said Prakash.

'Nothing is perfect.'

'But perfect to me is what you will appreciate so I have to chisel it to be a diamond.'

Our professor softened at this. The C.S.E. professor did not intervene.

'When will you give your presentation?'

'I will tell you Sir, before the last presentation is announced.'

'We'll meet next week, students,' wrapped up the professor and everyone left the room.

'You lied there. You had nothing at all,' I said to Prakash.

'Yes I lied. Sapana couldn't get the data. Now, I have time,' said Prakash.

'You don't need help?' asked Harsh.

'No.

On Saturday, I called Trisha at my home in the morning. My parents were to come back in the evening so I thought my place was the best for work. Together in my room, we sorted out the material.

'Thanks a lot Trisha,' I said.

'I knew you couldn't do it all by yourself.'

By eleven o' clock I had collected the material and Trisha had made some slides. She went to the bathroom. I heard a beep in Trisha's cell phone. I checked it and saw she had received a message.

Trisha came back a minute later and worked on the computer.

'Happy Birthday,' I wished her.

Trisha turned to face me. She looked surprised.

'I never told you that today was my birthday,' she said.

'I can't lie to you. You had left your phone and received a message. It said Happy Birthday. There was no name, only the phone number,' I said.

Trisha took the cell phone and checked it. She kept it in her pocket.

'You should have told me,' I said.

'It is no big deal. Everyone has a birthday.'

'Everyone is not Trisha. Come on, let's go out.'

'Look, it is nothing to be happy about,' Trisha said.

'You might not be, but I am.'

'I didn't bring any money today, sorry.'

I had saved some money lately to buy something. But, Trisha's happiness was important. She had helped me, after all.

'The treat is on me. We'll take an auto and go to Vasant Kunj.'

'I am supposed to give you treat, not the other way round,' said Trisha.

'You can give me a return gift someday,' I said.

I took an auto for Vasant Kunj from the main road. We reached the Central market and went to the Sagar Ratna restaurant to eat some South Indian food.

'Who sent the message?' I asked Trisha after we placed the order.

'Forget it. You will either laugh or won't believe it,' said Trisha.

'Try me.'

'Disha.'

I didn't laugh.

'But you are both so opposite, how come you are friends?' I said.

'You mean I am the non-studious bully and she is the bookworm, whom everyone calls the geek goddess. Right?'

'I didn't mean any of those things.'

'We are different and so we are good friends. She appreciates me for being cool. I appreciate her for being good at studies. But she isn't as bad as people think she is. She is nice.'

I ate a *masala dosa* while she settled for an *uthappam*, while we both had coffee.

Later I bought a cake from the bakery shop above and ate it on the steps.

'Black Forest. Do you think it is good?' I asked.

'Anything would be good,' she said.

We hung around and went back to my place at two.

Till four o' clock, we covered a lot of ground.

'I have pasted the raw matter on the slides. Edit it according to your need,' she said.

'Thanks a lot for helping me,' I said.

Trisha laughed.

'I should be thanking you for today. But I won't,' she said and left for her place.

Next Thursday, I was panicking. It was my presentation and I was very nervous.

Just before the presentation session, there was always a lot of commotion and activity. Four people had to give their presentations, so there were three more or less nervous souls roaming around the class. I sat in a corner quietly. I had given Dharm my U.S.B. drive to check if it was working fine. My PowerPoint file was in it. I checked the time. I had to go.

'Dharm, my U.S.B. drive,' I said.

Dharm had, unfortunately for himself, brought a laptop. So the rest three who had to give presentation also checked their U.S.B. drives on it. They all stood around Dharm.

'Leave everybody. I will give back your U.S.B. drives in the presentation room. Just go,' he said to them and all exited the classroom.

'Dharm. My presentation is the first,' I said to him.

'Of course, Suhaas. Which one is yours?' he asked.

I looked at the U.S.B. drives with him. There were six of them. And, four looked like mine. Black, with *Nevda* printed on them.

'How do you have these extra drives?' I asked.

'Three other people wanted some data from my laptop. Games and songs, etc. I shouldn't have brought this wretched thing in the first place,' said Dharm, cursing his laptop.

'Mine is one of the black drives. They all look alike,' I said.

'This is your drive,' said Dharm and picked up one.

'Come to the presentation room quickly,' I said to him and left.

Dharm had narrowly escaped punishment last time and he was not asked to give his presentation again.

I went to the presentation room and discovered that there was no C.S.E. professor. Lucky day, I thought. I had chosen Harsh as helper.

'Harsh, check the U.S.B. drive,' I said and gave him the drive.

The students were in their seats. The professor waited for me to start.

'It has a video file and a folder,' said Harsh after checking the drive.

I had downloaded a short video clip randomly from the Internet that showed how work in a telecom company takes place. It was just to generate interest in the audience. When Harsh told me about the video file I believed it was my drive. At that time I was busy looking at my notes and not on the computer screen or white screen behind me.

'Good morning, everyone. Before the presentation, I want to show a short clip about how work is done in any telecom company,' I said, looking at my audience.

'Is it necessary?' asked the professor, looking at his watch.

'Very necessary sir,' I said. I had to impress the audience in some way.

'Start the video,' I said to Harsh.

Harsh clicked on the mouse and without looking at the screen behind me, I began.

'As you can see, there is a lot of activity in this industry. This is how it all happens.

Please focus on the video,' I said as I looked at the professor.

Everyone's eyes were transfixed at the screen behind me. Their mouths were agape. The professor didn't blink an eyelid. Maybe the video was too good.

'This is generally how it all works, in any industry,' I said.

The professor still looked at the screen transfixed. But he spoke slowly.

'What is this?'

'I believe you can see it all clearly sir,' I said.

I saw Trisha. She was laughing. She gestured me to look behind and I saw the video on the white screen. I was stunned and petrified. I felt so hot as if I was inside a volcano. There was a lot of activity in the video for sure. It was after all, a porn movie. There was no sound. Or maybe my ears were not working.

'What is the meaning of this?' shouted the professor.

With that, I came back to my senses. I couldn't believe what was happening.

'Are you listening to me boy?' the professor shouted at the top of his voice.

'Yes,' I said as I tried to become normal. I looked at Harsh.

'Close the video,' I said and he closed it.

The professor didn't say anything. That gave me time to think. How did it happen?

'It's not my USB drive,' I explained.

'It is not yours?' asked the professor.

'No sir. I accidentally exchanged it with this similar looking U.S.B. drive. Give me a minute sir.'

'Suhaas, you are giving your presentation next week,' said the professor.

'Huh?'

'Figure out where it is. I am giving you last chance. Next week. And if I see such carelessness again, I'll take a serious action,' said the professor.

I sat in the last seat, away from everyone. The other three students gave their presentations. Two had similar black drives so they checked them and they were correct. After the presentation session, I stepped out. I saw Dharm.

'Man, whose U.S.B. drive did you give?'

'I am sorry. Trisha also gave me her U.S.B. drive and it was also black. Your drive got exchanged with hers. I gave her your drive by mistake,' said Dharm.

'Oh, god. I screwed it,' I said as I left Dharm behind.

'No you didn't,' said Trisha as she came behind me.

'You! Just because of you, I looked like some pervert. Is this the return gift for your birthday? You did not say once in the hall that it was yours and given me mine,' I said.

'If I would have given it to you there and then, everyone including the professor would know it was my drive.'

I looked angrily. Trisha laughed.

'Look at the brighter side. You got a whole week to prepare,' she said.

After she said that, my anger subsided.

'I can't believe you watch porn. And, carry it in a U.S.B. drive to the college,' I said.

'I just took it today from some friend. Besides, just because I am a girl, doesn't mean I can't watch porn. I am a human being too and it is part of being normal.'

'There was no sound so I didn't notice the video while speaking to students.'

'Our computers don't have speakers. Otherwise the noise would have reached outside. That wouldn't have been good.'

I didn't want to talk to her. My day had been wasted.

'How can I make it up to you?' she asked.

'Forget it. The damage is done.'

'Oh come on. Everyone believes the drive was not yours. This Saturday, there will be only you and me. I'll give you a treat. I also have to give you your return gift,' she said.

'I don't need any,' I said.

'Saturday is fixed. We are meeting at the Sahara Mall. Okay?' she said.

As if I could say no to her. I nodded.

On Friday morning, Trisha sat next to me in the first lecture.

'We are bunking. Today,' she said.

'After this lecture?' I asked.

'Yeah, and we'll come back directly on Monday,' she said.

'But we had it fixed for Saturday,' I said.

"Be adventurous. Can't you be absent for one day?' she said.

We jumped over the wall like I had in the second semester. An hour and a half later, we reached Sahara Mall. Trisha wanted to watch a movie.

She was keen to buy the tickets, after which we entered the movie hall. The movie started. There was a lot of action and suspense all the way and I was glued to the movie till intermission. I went outside with Trisha to buy some more popcorn. We came back. The action begun again. Machine guns, futuristic battle ships and what not. I was happily stuck to the wholesome entertainer when I was distracted by Trisha. She tried to whisper in my ear.

'Could you please keep quiet and watch the movie?'

She was taken aback by my sudden authority and munched quietly on the popcorn.

Few minutes later, Trisha nudged me. I looked at her and missed a bomb explosion on the screen.

'What is it?' I shouted angrily.

'Here, want shhome popcorn?' Trisha asked, holding a flake of popcorn gently between her lips.

'No,' I said and she went back to munching her popcorn.

Later, we had lunch. I ate *chole bhature* whereas she stuck to her burger. In the end, she had sauce all over her lips.

'Do I have something on my lips?' she asked.

'No.'

'I think its sauce. Can you remove it?'

'You have the tissue paper beside you Trisha,' I said and she grumbled and used it.

Around two o' clock, we stepped out of the mall. The weather was cloudy and it meant rain.

'It was a great day. You didn't really have to pay for anything,' I said happily.

Trisha looked sad. She stared at her shoelaces.

'Why such a long face? Is something wrong?' I asked.

Trisha looked at me. I saw she was furious. And also, her fists were clenched.

'Tell me Trisha.'

'You think it's about the movie or the food or that I want to get even to you? You are a fool, you don't know anything. Why do you act so innocent? Don't you get it?' shrieked Trisha.

The people around looked at us.

'Go inside and enjoy. Don't stand here,' said Trisha and everyone went inside.

'Trisha, you've been acting so strangely today. Did something happen?'

Trisha came closer to me.

'You didn't get one single thing. You didn't know why I asked you to eat popcorn. You didn't get why I asked you to remove the sauce. Any idiot would have understood,' she pouted.

I came closer to her and took out a handkerchief.

'Here, I have removed the sauce,' I said and wiped whatever little sauce I could see.

She looked directly into my eyes. She came so close that I couldn't see anything but her face.

'What?' I said but she didn't wait.

She kissed me and didn't allow me to unglue. It was a kiss of unmatched passion. I tried to part our lips but she didn't let me. She held my hands very tightly. And then I felt my whole body hit by giant wet drops.

'Trisha,' I said as I moved away to catch some breath.

'That was your return gift,' she said as she moved closer again.

'No Trisha. This is wrong, you are ruining our friendship.'

'You are ruining the moment,' she said and tried to kiss again but I moved away.

'What is wrong with you Trisha? We are friends,' I shouted. The little drizzle a few minutes back turned into a ferocious downpour. I stood shivering.

'So this means you don't know me. You are innocent, foolhardy and imperfect.

You can't match my fighting skills, but you bring a cake for me and ask me if I like it or   not. You are so cute. Everyone saw the bully, the tomboy in me. No one ever saw the girl in me. No one has ever spent his savings on me like that Suhaas. I don't know what more to tell you,' said Trisha.

She was getting wet too. Even if she was tough and manly, I doubted her skin could resist the cold and wet raindrops.

'Can I give more proof to you?'

'It is raining Trisha, let's go back home.'

'Answer me Suhaas. Do you not like me?'

'You know my past Trisha. My relationships don't last. You will repent it,' I said.

'After you told me your past, I know you completely. Do you think I am Simran and use you after knowing your past? Come on Suhaas, you know that much about me.'

I had nothing to say. But I understood Trisha. No girl had ever cared for me more.

I came closer to her and put my arms around her.

'I don't think any girl has liked me more. And well, I like you too. So, I take the risk of liking each other and hope you don't ditch me or betray me.'

She smiled back.

'I want to kiss you but I'd appreciate if we get out of this rain,' I said and she laughed.

Coincidentally, Prakash and my presentations were earmarked for the same day. After our presentations had been delayed, it was appropriate that we both presented together.

Prakash gave the most astounding presentation ever. He said that he had been working every day in the training. He described as to how his employee told about the company. He showed pictures of the office where he supposedly worked and not once did he hesitate. He linked one thing to another and though the link appeared absurd, it all seemed true with his glib salesman talk, smooth like his fake certificate.

'I don't know if what you say is real. But I want it to be. Good presentation,' said the professor. The C.S.E. professor had permanently opted out of the presentation room and simply vanished.

I gave my best presentation, explaining it all properly without faltering. I didn't know before, but all that I needed to boost my confidence was one solid kiss from Trisha.

'Good, at least this time we have no 'untoward' activity,' said the professor and everyone laughed including the professor himself.

After the presentation session got over, we all came out. Nothing went wrong that day and we were all cheery. There was something pleasant in the air. Prakash and I congratulated each other. When Harsh and Prakash busily talked to each other, Trisha gave me a peck on the cheek and went to the lab. Harsh and Prakash turned to face me and I hurriedly wiped off the lipstick.

'What happened?' asked Harsh.

'Nothing. Some dirt on my face,' I replied and we all walked towards the lab.

We had just reached the door of our lab when a girl stepped out of the lab next to us.

She looked at us and advanced in our direction. I didn't want her to be there. Harsh knocked his fist on the wall. Prakash just stared at her.

'Hi, Prakash,' beamed Anu.

❑

THE SIXTH SEMESTER

Jobs! Placements! Package! These were the terms we had never heard of before. And until the sixth semester, we had never known this strange creature called TPO or Training Placement Officer.

On the first day of our Sixth Semester, the TPO called all the third year students and showed us charts that depicted how the number of students who had got placed in a company had gone down over the past four years.

For the private companies that selected our college students for placement, there were a number of rounds to be cleared. The first round was a written aptitude test. The next round was usually a group discussion, followed by an interview.

So, the subject books were replaced by aptitude books and sample interviews downloaded from the Internet. The Placement Fever was at its peak.

'This is crazy, man,' bellowed Harsh one day.

'I am busy noting down websites to get previous years' question papers of various companies, every day,' said Prakash.

'Will any company visit our college?' I asked.

'No Suhaas, we will have to go to another college for the company exam. A company usually comes for two or three colleges, but our college can't accommodate them due to the space constraint soon,' said Harsh.

'You guys talk, I'll be back,' said Prakash and walked over to the restroom.

The moment Prakash disappeared, Harsh, encroached upon the topic that was so dear to his heart.

'How did Anu dare to speak to Prakash?' said an angry Harsh.

'Her mind changed a lot after she broke up with Prakash.'

After my presentation the three of us reached the lab, when the unexpected happened. Anu willingly came forward and said 'Hi' to Prakash, who did not respond. He rushed inside the lab, Harsh and I followed suit. We left her standing aloof outside the lab and she never returned.

'How do you know her feelings?' asked Harsh, coming back to the present..

I told Harsh about my conversation with Anu.

'Prakash is not the only one who made a mistake,' said Harsh.

'You want to talk about Trisha?' I asked.

'I had noticed her motivating Dharm to fight the Prof. You will get in trouble one day too,' said Harsh.

'So this is not about her loving me or not, rather about some pre-conceived notion in your head.'

Harsh gestured his disapproval, but I continued.

'Look, she is perfect. She likes me, I like her. That's it.'

Harsh looked at me and then at Prakash who had just come out of the toilet.

'Let's end this discussion here,' he said and we all went for lunch.

Trisha was full of surprises. One day, after college was over, she wanted me to come with her to her flat in Gurgaon. It wasn't her parents' home, but she was living there on rent with three other girls.

'Let's hurry up and get an auto,' I said.

'I have brought my motorbike,' she said.

I looked at her bike. It was surely a jazzy sports bike.

I sat at the back as she handed me a helmet. It felt strange to be a pillion rider, with a girl driving the bike. She kicked the bike to life and it roared and we were soon burning rubber and gas. Well, I was feeling hotter than the bike. After half an hour of crazy driving, the flying machine screeched to a halt in front of her apartment. She rang the doorbell. The door was opened by a girl in mini-shorts.

'Hey Trisha, who is this guest?' asked the Hot Pants.

'No guest,' explained Trisha said.

'Welcome Suhaas,' said the girl as she closed the door behind us.

Trisha took me straight to her room. Two guitars, one acoustic and other electric, were lying on the bed. Her desk was piled up with CDs of myriad rock artistes. The walls were adorned with huge posters of a number of rock bands. She was surely passionate about rock.

'I don't knowif it is a mere coincidence, but your passion for rock is very similar to that of Harsh,' I said.

I thought that Trisha might jump on hearing that or look impressed. All she said was, 'Yeah, maybe,' and that sounded disinterested.

'Come here, sit with me,' said Trisha.

I sat with her on her bed and she pulled me closer. We kissed and I forgot about asking any more questions.

'Best of luck,' Harsh said to me on the day of our first written test.

'You too,' I said.

Our first company had decided to visit our college, and the placement was meant only for our students. I pulled a blank when I read the question paper. I had no inkling about the technical questions, though I was somewhat conversant with the questions pertaining to aptitude. But as the paper was objective, I attempted all the questions provided in the paper, even those I didn't know. I looked at Prakash on the right. He mumbled *eeny meeny mini mo* and randomly marked an option.

He looked at me and gestured that he had no idea of the paper. Harsh, however, did look serious. Trisha didn't even look bothered. I looked at her friend Disha. Her head swung like a pendulum, to and fro, from the question paper to the solution paper. After one and a half hour, everyone in the room heard someone snoring at the back. We looked at a worn out student who had completely fallen asleep.

'Have to pass this, have to pass this…' he mumbled in his sleep.

'Get up boy, you are disturbing everyone,' said the invigilator.

'I am going to ace this!' he shouted in his sleep.

The invigilator went up to the student and tried to shake him from his slumber.

'I checked the sample question papers of the company. They have trick questions, funny questions. Their answers are not what they seem…' he mumbled in his sleep and started snoring again.

That caught every student's attention. Everyone looked back to their questions and rubbed the previous answers with erasers. When I didn't know the original answers, how would I change them?

'There is another thing…' the boy yelled in his sleep.

Everyone hung on to hear the next word. But then he started snoring again. From then on, all through the paper, he yelled different meaningless statements. Also some shocking ones.

'I proposed to a girl when I was 16. Then I found out she was married.'

'I stole a gun from my dad's drawer. It was cool.'

It was difficult to do the paper with the constant interruptions from the sleeping boy.

'I love you Heena!,' he mumbled and slept back again.

'What!' shouted a girl at the end of the room and then the girl sitting behind him got up. She slapped the boy on the cheek hard. That did the trick. The boy woke up with a start.

'What happened?' he asked, looking around.

'You cheat! You said you loved me,' said the girl who had slapped him again.

Heena, the girl at the end of the room, looked down embarrassed and carried on with her paper.

'Boy, please go outside. You clearly have no energy for this paper and you are disturbing the entire class,' said the invigilator.

'Sir, I haven't slept for days because of this paper. I have to get this job, no matter how,' he said.

'Please leave. You must have ticked some answers.'

So the boy left the class, and the rest of the students fiddled with the questions for fifteen more minutes. The bell rang. We went outside and saw the worn out, exhausted boy.

'Hi, my name is Suhaas. I have never seen you,' I said.

'I am from the other section,' said the boy.

'I know him. He is Shashi,' said Harsh.

'What happened to you?' I asked.

'I don't know. I slept and Reena slapped me. I had been studying day and night. And on the D-day, I fell asleep,' said Shashi.

'You have been talking in sleep. You made us change our answers. You told a lot of your secrets. You said you loved Heena,' I said.

'I am ruined, destroyed,' screamed Shashi and left us.

'He didn't even give us a chance to console him,' said Harsh.

'So, how was your paper?' I asked.

'Frankly, I am not sure. I changed my answers after Shashi's mumbling,' said Harsh.

'Mine was bad,' I said.

Prakash stood by our side.

'I randomly marked any answer. I attempted the whole paper,' said Prakash.

'We will know the results within three hours,' said Harsh.

And we sure did. None of us passed the written test, which was not everyone's cup of tea.

'I am not sitting for any written test anymore,' said Prakash.

But he sure did, as did everyone else. None of us passed in the second test or even the third test. The biggest problem was that we had no mock written papers for the companies we had to sit for. Those who did and reached the interview stage were not really happy. The conditions of the companies were ridiculous and so was the pay scale. They opted out.

'I am fed up of all this. I am playing the guitar and performing in the cultural festival in mid April,' said Prakash one day.

'What about jobs and companies?' I asked.

'We'll sit for whatever companies come for us, but we are not going to make placement a pressure point,' declared Prakash.

In early March, one company wanted to recruit students from three colleges, including ours. However, the criterion was 73% marks and above. The exam was to be held in a college in a far off district in Haryana. Harsh was eligible, but Prakash and I weren't. On a cold morning, we met Harsh in the canteen. He was going in the chartered bus along with the other candidates and the exam was to take place the next day.

'Best of luck, Harsh! You have to compete with fewer people. So who all are going?' asked Prakash.

'Students from CSE, ECE and IT are eligible. The college is stuffing everyone in a single bus,' said Harsh.

'Don't be nervous, you do have lots of grey matter under that black mop of yours,' said Prakash.

'Okay guys, ring me up tomorrow,' said Harsh.

'Sure, bye!' we waved to him as he boarded the jam-packed bus.

After the bus left the college campus, we bought sandwiches and ate away to glory, sitting on a sunny bench.

'You must be happy,' said Prakash.

'Yes, Harsh will surely get selected,' I said.

'I am talking about Trisha,' said Prakash.

'Harsh told you?' I asked.

'He did not tell me anything, but I know. You must be looking forward to spending some time together,' said Prakash.

'Any objections?'

'No, its fine with me,' said Prakash.

'Thanks! I feel like bunking college today,' I said.

So, Trisha and I bunked college and went to the malls and then shopped a couple of things. We proceeded to her apartment and she showed me the stuff she bought.

'I got something for you,' I told her.

'What?'

'This,' I said and showed her a rock band T-shirt.

'Do you like it?' I asked.

She examined it for one whole minute.

'I hate this band and the colour. I will give it to someone else.'

'As you wish,' I said, disappointed.

I sat on her bed as she put it in her cupboard. My gaze fell on the middle drawer of her desk. It was slightly open. I placed my hand on its handle.

'Don't touch it!' shouted Trisha.

'I was just looking.'

'Don't touch it ever.'

I didn't touch it. But, I felt curious about it.

It was the next day, the day of the written test for Harsh and the others in the bus. We had called him at nine in the morning through my cell phone. Harsh didn't sound right. His paper was supposed to start at ten.

Harsh's voice at the other end of the line was unclear.

'They didn't let us in,' he said.

'What do you mean they didn't let you in?' I asked.

'Put the cell phone on speaker,' Prakash said to me.

I switched on the loud speaker.

'When we reached the host college around seven thirty and asked the guard, he didn't let us in. A professor came out and we told him that our college was also contesting for the company. The professor said our college was not in the list,' said Harsh.

'Not in it? But why did our college send all you people there?' I asked.

'I don't know. The professors called the TPO at eight a.m. His assistant attended the call and said he was busy lecturing the fourth year students. We tried to call him again, but his cell phone was switched off.' said Harsh.

'Why don't they just let you all take the exam? You wouldn't have come all the way without proper eligibility,' said Prakash loudly.

'The host college authorities want to talk to our TPO only. But he is not picking up the phone. I'll talk to you guys later,' said Harsh and hung up.

'This is bad,' said Prakash.

'The TPO has to clear the air,' I said.

'Let's attend our lectures and call him during lunch,' said Prakash.

But Harsh didn't pick up our calls for the rest of the day. Only the next day did we come to know what actually happened. Harsh boarded my college bus in the morning. I was surprised to see him and wanted to ask him about what happened. He said he would tell me and Prakash together. We met Prakash and Harsh told us everything in the canteen.

'I am sorry guys, but by afternoon, my cell phone battery got exhausted. We were not allowed to take the exam despite our repeated protests. It looks like the company had informed our college. Some representative from our college was supposed to come at least a day before the exam and register our college name in the list of the host college. But, no one from our college registered the name. May be no one in the college knew, but no one bothered to find out. By the evening, we were sick of pleading. So we all went back to the bus. The driver dropped us all at our bus stops. Hence, I came in my usual bus today,' said Harsh.

'It's really sad,' sympathized Prakash.

'Get out you idiot. You can't pick up the phone. But at least you can hear us.'

Prakash, Harsh and I exchanged looks at hearing those words.

'Who is shouting?' asked Prakash.

'It is Akhil. He also went with me to that college yesterday,' said Harsh and we three ran to the source of the sound.

'Come out now,' shouted Akhil.

It was crazy. All the students who had gone with Harsh the day before stood in the prayer ground, right below the TPO's office window on the first floor. While Akhil shouted at the top of his voice, others joined in chorus.

'They look angry,' I said.

'Yes, won't they wonder where you are?' Prakash asked Harsh.

As soon as he said that, one of the boys in the group noticed us standing a few feet away.

'Harsh! Come here. We are protesting for yesterday's mishap,' the boy was calling Harsh.

Everyone walked towards us.

'Forget it Akhil,' said Harsh.

'We have to take a stand. We can't take this lightly,' said Akhil.

'It concerns not only us, but every student who fights for placement. All third year students should boycott the classes and go for a strike,' said Shashi.

His words aroused interest in the group. I hated Shashi.

'We will sit in the college ground,' said a boy.

The third year students were on STRIKE.

After half an hour, all the third year students flooded the college ground. Akhil sat ahead of the whole group.

'You are second in command,' Akhil told Harsh. Harsh looked behind at me. And then back at Akhil. I sat with Prakash and some Mechanical students.

Around nine, a professor came out to meet us.

'What is happening?' he asked Akhil.

'We are protesting for what happened yesterday in that college for placement. Unless someone tells us how it happened, we are not attending any classes,' he said.

'Is this another strike?' asked the professor.

'It sure is,' said Akhil.

He went inside and no one came out until the last lecture. The computer H.O.D. met us.

'Come inside all of you. The TPO wants to talk to you,' he said.

We all sat in the auditorium. All the Professors stood in a single file on the stage. As soon as the TPO ascended the stage, the students booed.

'Stop behaving like hooligans,' shouted the TPO.

'Silence people. Please, let him speak,' said Vinay sweetly.

The auditorium fell silent.

'I know you want an explanation for yesterday's happenings. I accept that we were at fault. We did not register ourselves, as the professors with you have told me. I am really sorry,' apologized the TPO.

Several people stood up and yelled out in an asynchronous manner.

'Sorry is not enough. We lost a good job.'

'Good companies are rare for us. I can't believe you can put our careers at stake.'

'I want to address the students who are concerned with yesterday's incident. Not the rest. They may go,' said the TPO.

'Why? This affects us all,' shouted a student.

'Show me your face,' said the TPO.

The student got up. It was Shashi.

'I know you. You were not even eligible for the company yesterday,' said TPO.

'I speak for the rest of us. If we go to a distant college and the same thing happens, what will happen to us?'

'I was told to discuss yesterday's issue with specific students. Nothing happened to the rest of you,' said the TPO.

'The issue is larger than yesterday,' said Akhil.

'Did you go there yesterday?' asked the TPO.

'Yes. I was disappointed. First thing, can you tell me why you didn't pick up your phone yesterday?' asked Akhil.

'I was busy. I was giving lectures and attending meetings,' TPO said.

'Well, we came back in the evening. Even if you called late, we would have received your call.'

The TPO didn't know what to say. He couldn't have yelled at Akhil for expressing his anger.

'We had protested only for yesterday. But as all of us have gathered here, there are many things for us to say,' said Akhil.

The TPO looked on. He took a chair and sat down. The professors sat on the stage.

'Forget yesterday. You had told us that 60 companies asked for third and fourth year students when we were in the first year. Today, we should be having more companies as our college is the oldest in Gurgaon. On the contrary, for us, that is the ECE students, four major companies have called us this year,' said Akhil.

'Just four? There were so many companies after that,' said the TPO when Akhil stopped him.

'Please, sir. The four companies that came were the main ones.

And the rest were either third rate companies or BPOs. Top colleges have large number of companies that come and every student is not selected by the first company. We, who know will have lesser placements, should have maximum opportunities. The charts you showed to lure us to become a student of your college are crap. Meaningless,' he said.

Everyone nodded. The TPO seemed lost. He asked for support from professors.

'We are not provided either mock papers or Group Discussion hints. We are unprepared for companies that come.'

'They are right sir,' said a professor.

The other professors nodded.

'I will try my best to resolve the problems. But please don't strike again,' he said and left the auditorium. So did the professors and the rest of us.

I chatted with Harsh the next day. Prakash was absent.

'I have decided that I am not going to make job a pressure point anymore,' said Harsh.

'What do you want?'

'I want to play the guitar in the cultural fest,' he said.

'Prakash also wants to. Go and talk to him. You both can form a band,' I said.

'Really? That would be great,' Harsh said.

In the evening in bus, Girish sat alone in the F-Row. It had changed and it comprised no more of fourth year students.

'Hi,' I said as I sat with him.

'You found time to meet me, huh? You sat with Trisha yesterday,' he said.

'Are you angry with me?' I asked.

'No. I don't feel like talking about it right now,' he said.

'Tell me Girish.'

'It's just the job stress. Very few good companies come for mechanical department. I always fail in the interviews for them. The rest offer low pay packages. I can't take it anymore,' he said.

'Don't worry warrior. We also have one more year to go,' I said.

However much I cheered him, I knew the reality. Lesser companies than in the previous years were recruiting students.

A few days later, Prakash, Harsh and I discussed in the canteen.

'Four years before, our college was the only private college in the region. Hence many companies were rapidly coming. Now many more colleges have mushroomed. There is stiff competition,' said Harsh.

'You said Girish was upset regarding something?' asked Prakash.

'Yes, regarding placement,' I said.

'AAAAAAAAAAAAAHHHHHHHHHH.'

All heads turned towards the source of the scream. It seemed quite painful.

'Who was that?' questioned Prakash.

'Let's check out,' said Harsh.

Everyone ran outside the canteen and towards the college ground. We all reached the spot of action. I couldn't believe it.

A boy was lying on the ground face down, writhing in pain. Another boy stood with a ripped shirt a bruised face.

'Girish,' I said as I recognized him.

'Get up you son of a bitch!' Girish shouted at the boy lying facedown. The boy did not even stir.

Harsh and Prakash went over to the boy. I hurried to be on Girish's side.

'He's breathing!' shouted Prakash.

'STILL?' shouted Girish.

'Come with me Girish,' I said in a low whisper.

'NO.'

'I SAID COME WITH ME!'

Girish was dumbfounded.

'We have to hurry! We have to take him to the hospital. Urgently,' said Prakash about the boy lying facedown.

'Okay, let me get some professor to take the boy quickly to the hospital,' said Harsh.

'I have to take Girish with me,' I said.

Vinay stepped out of the college building. Prakash and Harsh hurried and told him everything. Vinay sat with them and the boy in his car. The car exited the college gate and was gone.

'Please everyone, don't tell anyone about this fight. Just keep it to yourself,' I said to the crowd.

Girish's shirt was a mess. I dragged him along with me to the restroom. The boys inside were stunned as they looked at Girish.

'Please guys hurry up and leave,' I said.

Everybody hurriedly left. I opened the tap and forcibly placed Girish's head under the running water.

'Here, wear this shirt, take my napkin and throw it anywhere. I'll come back with some bandage,' I said.

I exited the restroom and hurried to the chemistry laboratory. I found some band-aid, cotton and cloth. I came back and placed a band aid on his scar and covered the knuckles of his right hand with bandage. After all the covering, I dragged him out of the restroom and dashed towards the college gate.

'*Bhaiyya*,' I said to the guard, 'This boy is really ill. I have to take him home.'

The guard took pity and we exited the gate. I rushed to my home. I opened the door with the keys.

'Have some water,' I said and offered a glass to Girish.

'Seems like you need to give an explanation,' I told him clearly.

'Looks like I messed up,' said Girish calmly.

'LOOKS LIKE?'

'I was tensed after failing in yet another interview. I headed for the canteen, when I brushed past him in the college ground. He got angry and insulted me. He said that I was a loser as I couldn't get placed in a company. He is a second year mechanical student. I couldn't take insult from my junior,' Girish defended himself.

'Prakash' flashed on my cell phone display as it rang. I picked it up.

'He's okay,' said Prakash, 'the boy is in a Gurgaon hospital. Where is Girish?'

'Girish is with me. I took him home,' I said.

'Suhaas, don't bring Girish here or anywhere near college. If Girish has a cell phone, tell him to switch it off.'

'OK. What should I do?'

'You come here to the hospital. Vinay is with us. We have to talk to the boy.'

'OK.'

'So?' asked Girish.

'The boy is OK. I am going to meet him.'

Girish watched me as I walked to the door.

'And one more thing,' I said to him.

'What?' he asked.

I punched him in the face hard. And I hit him on his knee. Girish yelped in pain.

'Good. But get a few band aids and bandage. You need to look equally damaged,' I said as I left the room.

I met Vinay at the hospital.

'I can't believe Girish did it,' he said.

'Sir, both of them are at fault,' I explained to Vinay.

'Don't explain it to me. His parents will ask and so will the principal.'

'Please listen to me Vinay. You have to help us. We have to change the story.

Girish did not fight alone, few third year students kicked the boy too. They left as they saw people come out of the canteen. So the damage was not done by Girish alone,' I said.

'I am not supporting you in any lie,' said Vinay clearly.

'This is a question of Girish's career and life. The principal and the boy's parents will listen to you,' I said.

Vinay sighed.

'I can't believe what all I do for you guys, for the sake of your career,' said Vinay.

'Thank you!' I said and went inside the boy's ward.

Harsh and Prakash were sitting there. The boy rested on a bed. He was lying there with his hand in a sling around his neck. His face bore some visible signs of being beaten up. There was a band aid on his forehead.

'Can he walk? ' I asked.

'Yes. No disfigurations anywhere. Only superficial injuries,' said Harsh.

I looked directly into the boy's eyes.

'What is your name?' I asked.

'Arvind,' he said.

'Listen to me Arvind. You just dealt with our best friend, who would normally not hurt even a fly, but kicked your ass today. So there is a serious fault on your side,' I said.

He opened his mouth to speak but I raised my hand and he kept his mouth shut.

'Tell me one thing. Was anybody around there before the fight started?' I said.

'No. Only after we fought did students rush to see us.'

'You are going to tell anyone who asks you that you provoked Girish into a fight. Some passersby joined the fray. They battered you up and ran away. You stay with this story or be ready to face the consequences,' I said.

'Who are you to order me? I will tell what I want to the principal, who will certainly favour me,' boasted Arvind.

'He will not. You know why? You didn't fight with Girish, you messed with us. I know there are a lot of rumours floating around the college about you. So do as I say,' I said and got up.

Arvind became silent. I sounded like a mafia boss with his two henchmen. Prakash and Harsh looked at me. We walked towards the exit.

'You know what he did?' whispered Harsh.

'No. At home, Girish told me he had heard rumours about the boy. Arvind's silence confirms the rumours are true.'

As soon as I, Prakash and Harsh were about to exit, the boy shouted.

'Fine. I will do it. But there was a girl who intervened.'

'Who are you talking about?' I asked.

'She was around there when our fight had started. A tomboy girl in a rock band shirt. She shouted at Harsh to tear me apart and that is when he came into the mood and started beating me. She disappeared as soon as everyone came running. You know her?'

Harsh and I exchanged looks.

'I know no such person,' I said and left with my friends.

I reached my home and saw Trisha sitting next to Girish.

'What happened?' asked Girish. He had covered his entire body with bandages.

'Don't overdo it. You can go back home in the evening. Here is the plan,' I said and told him all that I had told Arvind.

'Who would be these guys?' asked Girish.

'You don't know. That is why they are not from mechanical. They could be anyone from our bus,' I said.

Harsh looked at Trisha. I felt uneasy.

'Did you propel Girish to fight?' he asked.

'What?' Trisha answered, showing a baffled expression.

'That boy saw and heard you.'

'It is a lie,' said Trisha.

'She was not there,' said Girish.

'You are protecting her because she is Suhaas' girlfriend. She could have ruined your life,' Harsh said to him.

'I told Girish I would kill the boy if he didn't hit him. I couldn't see Girish being talked to like that by a junior,' said Trisha angrily.

I was horrified to look at the fire in her eyes.

'Or shoot him with a gun, isn't it?' asked Harsh wildly.

Trisha looked stunned. She clutched her band shirt.

'You will never change Trisha.'

Trisha cried. She ran out of the front door and left the house.

Girish sat quietly. I told Harsh to come with me to the balcony.

'Harsh, you really need to tell me what is going on,' I said.

'I know Trisha even before she joined college,' said Harsh.

'Since when?'

'I shifted to a new school in seventh class. It was then that I met Trisha in my class.

She was a lonely girl with no friends and was mostly involved in fights. I don't know why, but I befriended her. I got to know of her terrible father, who used to slap her every day and had no respect for his wife or kids. She said that she could not do anything. I guess that her violent nature towards others was a natural reaction. When we were in eighth, her dad got transferred abroad. With his absence, she became better. I introduced her to rock music and we became best friends. She didn't fight anymore.

In Class Nine, she had made friends with some classmates. Everything was fine until one day when we both were in the basketball court. We were alone except for our classmate Bhoj who was trying to hit the basket. A boy came to the basketball court. His name was Saahil and he was mean. He tried to snatch the ball away from Bhoj. I tried to resolve the dispute but Saahil didn't let go of Bhoj. Just then, Trisha came with her bag. She told Bhoj to hit Saahil and I was shocked at her words. She placed her hand inside her bag and pulled out a gun. She pointed it at Saahil.'

I stood there, stumped, with my eyes on Harsh.

'A gun?' I uttered in sheer disbelief.

'I had the same look in my eyes as you have now. I mean, we were all in ninth class. All of us stared at the gun in her hand. Saahil was petrified. He let go of Bhoj's collar. I snatched the gun from Trisha's hand. I ran after him and stopped him. I apologized on Trisha's behalf but Saahil was scared. He never told the incident to anyone. But since that day, Trisha and I have avoided each other. After the results of ninth class, Saahil and Trisha left school. I never contacted them and hoped to never see them again.

When I came to this college and saw Trisha, those memories became fresh. She avoided me and so did I. I even changed my section to be with you and Prakash. When you and Trisha became a couple, I thought she had changed. But after what she said to Girish, I am sure that she didn't change. I can never trust her with my friends,' said Harsh.

Harsh had expressed his feelings frankly, but I didn't want to believe any of it.

'I will talk to Trisha,' I said and went back to check on Girish.

I took Girish to my home and the principal had called his parents. Girish and his parents, Arvind and his parents; I, Harsh, Prakash, Vinay and principal met a few days later. Arvind left out Trisha and told the story as I had told him. He was suspended for a week.

He and his parents were told to leave. Vinay was summoned. Vinay told that he had seen two other boys hitting Arvind and running away. I, Harsh and Prakash supported Girish, who also got away with two weeks of suspension. Later, Vinay told me he would never lie again. Girish hugged me and was happy not to be thrown out of college.

After a week, I was able to finally confront Trisha. I met her and told her what Harsh had said.

'Is it true?' I asked.

'Yes,' said Trisha.

'I am not angry at anything Trisha. I just wish you had told me the truth.'

'It was an angry, terrible past. It is an incident I do not cherish. I did change. When I came to college, I had no intention of making people fight. But I hold true responsibility of what happened with Girish. Yes, I did become angry. But I wasn't going to pull out a gun,' she said.

'Why did you act that way in school?' I asked and she explained.

'The day before the incident, my dad came home. Instead of loving me, he slapped me. He was still, the same asshole. Without his knowledge, I stole his licensed revolver that night and kept it in my bag. I was so angry that I wanted to shoot him with it someday. The next day to school, after I saw Saahil with Bhoj, a sort of unknown and unexpected rage flared in me. The rest, as you know is history. I was shocked with myself. Since then, I didn't dare to face Harsh, Bhoj or Saahil. After my ninth class, I left my rotten dad with my mom and changed home. I lived as a paying guest in another city, and studied in another school. I never talked to my dad but my mother paid for me, because she wanted to. Since my tenth class, I have never met my dad and never came back home. Since my second year in college, I have not met my parents or contacted them, but my mother sends me money for my expenses. I was always tough and ready to fight. But what I said to Girish was momentary. I guess Harsh is right. I became as angry as I was on the day of the gun incident. Maybe the past had risen in me. I still have that gun today. It is in the drawer that I didn't want you to touch.'

That is why she didn't want me to come near the drawer.

'Trisha. Now, it is all in the past,' I said.

'No Suhaas. I have avoided my father for years. I have avoided my best friend, who thinks I am a violent maniac. I have to face them and only then I can meet you.'

'Don't we like each other?'

'I know we do. But if Harsh is right, I need some time to understand myself and remove my fears. Till then, I cannot face you,' said Trisha.

With that, she left me in the class alone. After half an hour, I left the class and went to the old library that was never reconstructed. I took out a rope from an old dusty cupboard and hung it around the high fan. I tied the knot and made a noose at the end of the rope firmly. I raised the rope till it hung in mid-air.

I took a chair and stood on it, with the rope in my hands. I took the noose in my hands. Just then, the door of the library opened. Harsh entered with Prakash.

'What are you both doing here?' I asked.

'I just came here to talk to Harsh alone. I didn't expect you to be here. Are you hanging yourself?' he asked casually.

'Yes, I am.'

'Don't be mad, get down now,' said Harsh.

I was about to place the noose around my neck, when Harsh kicked my chair away. I fell down and hurt my knee.

'My knee hurts, you idiot.'

'You would have been dead. What is wrong with you?' he asked.

'You decided to hate Trisha and never be friends with her. Trisha felt ashamed and left me. Now let me die in peace,' I said.

I went back and placed the chair in its proper position.

'Trisha did what she had to,' said Harsh.

'No one cares about my feelings. Goodbye,' I said and walked to the library door.

'Will you try to commit suicide again?' asked Harsh.

'No. I don't believe in poison, the rope is hanging on the fan and the gun is at Trisha's home. So sorry to disappoint you, but no,' I said as I left the library.

From that day on, everyone adjusted to the fact that Trisha was not talking to me anymore. I only talked to Harsh and Prakash.

Besides what happened to me, they all did have one thing in Common-Rock. So in April, on the first day of cultural fest, Prakash and Harsh were performing with their band.

There was a huge crowd that day and I saw Trisha too. Maybe she could not face Harsh or me, but she could not resist the music. We were all at the same place. I was ready to drown all my sorrows in the music. I looked at the seething sea of students dancing around me.

It was unbelievable. I never belonged to the Rock culture, but for many in the country, Rock was an instrument of Power. If I were Harsh, I would look at the guitar like King Arthur looked at the *Excalibur.* The crowds cheered as he slung the guitar strap round his neck.

He raised his right hand in the air and showed the 'devil horn' sign with his fingers. The crowd roared and raised their hands too. Not everybody knew Harsh. But the moment the spotlight hit him and the music echoed in the background, he became a *Rockstar*.

❑

THE SEVENTH SEMESTER

'Finally, we are in our last year. Our work load will become less,' said Prakash.

'And the job tension shall increase,' I said.

'Do you see us as tensed as you?' said Harsh.

One good thing happened was that Vinay became our professor for Intelligent Instrumentation or I.I.

'You seem sad,' Vinay said to me one day.

No one in the class wanted to study. So Vinay had told everyone to do whatever they wanted. I chose to talk to Vinay.

'What can you do about a break-up?' I blurted.

'Who broke up – she, you, or both?' asked Vinay.

'She did, for her own personal reasons, nothing to do with me, and said she needed time to think about it. It is my third break-up.'

'What happened in the first two cases?'

'With the first girl, someone else loved her much more and she had mistaken me for him. The second one simply made a fool of me. I loved the third girl, so I feel terrible now.'

'You never did cause a break-up, as a reason always existed. In the first case, it was the lover. In the second, it was the girl's greed. In the third case, it was her decision or rather indecision. The day you make a mistake and cause the break-up, that girl will be the girl for you.'

'You seem to know a lot.'

'Experience, man.'

A week later, I found an excuse to distract myself.

'It is a quiz on engineering. The preliminary round is day after tomorrow. And, the finals are two days later,' informed Prakash.

'Let us all go for it,' I said excitedly.

'One team can have only two students,' explained Harsh.

'You both want to be together?' I asked.

'No. One of us can be with you. But someone else needs to put in his or her name with one of us. Let us check whether someone has already put in our name or not,' said Prakash.

Prakash and Harsh set out to find a partner for themselves. I did want to participate, but only if my partner was one of them.

The next morning, both gave me the exact status.

'You are not paired with any of us,' said Harsh.

'Why?' I queried.

'It can't happen. Two students already paired our names with them before either of us could have paired with you,' said Prakash.

'Am I alone now?' I asked.

Prakash and Harsh exchanged glances. Finally Prakash said it.

'You are paired with Disha.'

'What are you talking about?' I asked, 'What if I don't pair up with her?'

'Then none of you remains in the quiz,' said Prakash.

'What if I find another partner?'

'Then you are in and Disha's out. I am sure a lot of people would be making groups today,' said Prakash.

'Fine' I said and I left him to begin my partner hunt, but none seemed interested. In short, my search was futile.

I got tired with my partner hunt and sat in the canteen. It was empty as the lectures were still going on. To my amazement, I saw

Disha, the geek goddess. She read a book and sat on a chair. She was the girl with the glasses and the ego.

I went up to her, but she didn't look up. I sat next to her.

'Uh, hello,' I said.

'Yes Suhaas.'

'I think by now you know that I am your quiz partner, by default.'

She didn't speak for a whole minute.

'Yes,' she said finally.

'Do you have a problem with it?'

'We can't do anything about it. Trisha got ill, so we are together now. It's only a quiz,' she said.

'Have you prepared for tomorrow?' I asked her.

'It is just the preliminary round. I don't need to. It's all up here,' she said, pointing to her brain.

She sure had it. For a one hour written preliminary, she marked the answers in twenty minutes. Our team was selected for finals, including four other teams. Except that none of them contained a familiar name. Not even Harsh and Prakash.

'Good work,' said Prakash to me in the third lecture.

'You aced it. Sorry bro, you will have to put up with the freak for another day,' said Harsh.

After the last lecture, Disha met me.

'You have to come with me. To my home,' she said.

'What for Disha?'

'I wouldn't feel like preparing for the stupid quiz if my team partner was not with me.'

I got it. She was a geek. She wanted to prepare intensively for a quiz.

My automatic response was 'OK.'

I told the situation to Harsh and Girish, who were surprised by Disha's attitude and the turn of events.

'You are not coming with us?' asked Harsh.

'I can't. I'll go in her bus,' I said.

Disha and I reached her home. Her apartment was on the ground floor. I walked into the house, but couldn't find a soul except her. Disha went straight to her room and shut the door. Just then, fortunately, her mother walked in with a tray containing a cup of tea and biscuits.

'Disha told me you were arriving, Suhaas. Have some snacks and tea,' she said.

'Thank you,' I said. I looked around. I saw photographs of Disha's mom with her daughter.

'When will Uncle reach home, aunty?' I asked.

'He divorced me years ago and got remarried,' said Disha's mother.

I prevented my cup from falling.

'I know what you are thinking. You have met her friend Trisha. She is not living with her father too. But at least her parents are together. She should forgive her father.'

I silently drank my tea. I preferred the monologue.

'I don't care if Disha is a success or failure in life. I want to see a smile on her face,' concluded Disha's mother.

'Everything will be fine aunty. I assure you.'

'Thank you.'

I thanked her for the tea and she headed back to kitchen.

'Took you time. What, mom caught you?' asked Disha when I entered her room.

'Just talking,' I said and sat with her on her bed.

Disha didn't answer and took out a book and started reading. She adjusted her glasses.

'Here,' she said and gave me a book regarding scientific explorations. Her room was full of books, charts and everything unfashionable. I focused on the book for a few minutes and then lost interest.

'Hey,' I said as my gaze fell on a book on her table. I picked it up and saw it.

'This is a fairytale book. Is it yours?' I asked.

Disha grabbed the book from me.

'Where did you find it?'

'On that table,' I said.

'The house cleaner must have found it.'

'Who gave it to you?'

I had asked a wrong question.

'Dad,' she said and hugged the book tight.

I watched as she dropped the book on her bed. Disha picked up a box from under the bed and opened it. She turned the other side, so I couldn't see her face. She opened the box. She took something in her hand and started crying. She had removed her glasses and her eyes were filled with tears. She was crying on a family photograph.

'That is my dad,' she said as she pointed to a man.

I picked up her glasses and said, 'You should wear them.'

'I don't need my glasses!'

'Please don't cry' I said and offered my handkerchief. She threw it away and put her head on my lap.

Now, that was weird.

'He left us when I was twelve. And I bungled up my life! I could concentrate on nothing. Although I got through the boards, I messed up my competitive exams and landed up in this stupid college, with no guarantee of the future. I work hard and try to top every exam so that I am eligible for any company that offers me a job. And then, on top of it, everyone hates me!' she told and cried even more.

For the first time in my life, some girl had opened her heart out like this to me. She could have been in a much better college.

I don't know what happened to me. I felt an instant urge to embrace her. I held her hand and she held mine tightly. She stopped crying. I came close to her, so close that I could see my reflection in her eyes. She froze. I edged closer to her and she did too. She pressed her lips against mine. And we kissed. I tried to remove my hand, but she held it tightly.

When we finally parted our lips, I sat there, panting. I got up from the bed.

'I must go. We'll talk about the quiz later,' I said and walked out of the door, not turning back even once.

'You did what!' Harsh exclaimed.

It was the next day at college. I narrated my story to Harsh.

'Were you freaking out of your mind? ' Harsh screamed.

'It was a weak moment. She was crying. None of us wanted it,' I said.

'She hasn't come today,' Harsh said.

'Maybe she is upset about what happened yesterday.'

Suddenly, I heard a buzzing sound on my cell phone. I got a message in my inbox.

It was from Disha.

Sorry, I am late today. I will attend the next lecture. Please meet me later in canteen.

'The geek she is, I presume she couldn't write a shorter message. But it's pretty,' Harsh commented sarcastically.

I felt like jamming the cell phone right between his teeth but controlled my emotions.

I felt more astonished at Disha's message than getting angry at Harsh.

I met her during lunch in the canteen.

'Hi' said Disha.

'We need to talk about last night.'

'It was the best night of my life.'

'What is wrong with you Disha? You should be mad at me,' I screamed.

'You're saying you didn't like the kiss?'

'You were crying and I was consoling you. But then you kissed me.'

'YOU wanted to kiss me. Just admit it.'

'It was momentary,' I justified.

She sulked and I realized the truth - a girl, whom I loathed, liked me.

'Do you like me Disha? Be frank!'

She did not speak. That meant yes.

'Disha, I do not know you. I broke up with Trisha just recently and I don't know what you want.'

'I understand.'

'Please understand.'

'We are still friends right? We have a quiz together,' she said.

'We will always be friends,' I told her and shook hands with her.

'Cheer up,' I said and she gave a wide smile. I knew she was trying hard not to cry.

The quiz, well, it seemed decided anyway. The whole class knew Disha was the Ms. Know-it-all. On the next day, the D-Day of the final quiz, I met her. We proceeded to the auditorium where the finals were to take place.

'And here is the first question to all our teams,' said the quizmaster cheerfully.

He asked the first, second, third question and so on. I wasn't prepared for the quiz.

More so, I wasn't prepared for the unexpected. Disha was hardly answering. I gave as many answers I could. We merely scraped through the first round. There was a ten minute break and everyone got up from their chairs. I stood up and found Disha still sitting.

'Get up Disha,' I said.

'What's happened to you?' I asked as soon as we got out of the auditorium.

'Dad called in the morning.'

Dad? I thought he was gone from her life.

'He had vanished like a ghost. And then I got a call in the morning from him. He scolded me for talking to his second wife's daughter in a bookstore. I remembered it was a week ago and I did not know who she was at that time.' she said.

I checked the watch. The quiz must have started, I thought.

'Go and wash your face,' I said.

She went to the girls' toilet. Few minutes later, she stepped out.

'How could he even talk to me like that?' Disha said.

'Disha' I said and I held her hands. She was taken aback.

'Let bygones be bygones, you are not responsible for your dad's behaviour. If he is nasty with you, it's his loss. You are precious,' I said.

Her spirits lifted.

'Let's go for the quiz. Now, I won't disappoint you,' said Disha.

That was really some change of mood. Disha scored the highest in the quiz. Not once or twice, but every time a question was asked. The teams that were under the false impression that Disha had lost her touch were simply wiped off. The rest was history.

'That was fun,' Disha said after the quiz was over. She held the trophy in both her hands as we walked.

'Yes, it was good.'

'Here, take this,' she said and gave me the trophy.

'You answered all the questions after the break.'

'But you helped me.'

Everyone said that Disha was a selfish girl. But that was untrue as, at that moment, she shared with me her joy, not just her trophy.

'So what is the deal with Disha?' asked Harsh the next day, in the canteen.

'She wants to be my friend. She talks nicely. I don't know why everyone hates her,' I said.

'You just want to be friends because she kissed you. She is a hateful bookworm,' opined Harsh.

'Don't combine things. Disha is a good girl and there are many reasons for her present attitude. Trisha broke up with me because of what she did. You don't know Disha,' I said.

'So, now you are at loggerheads with your best friend?'

'All I say is, don't judge someone you don't know,' I said.

Harsh stomped his feet and left the canteen. Prakash stood there.

'I hate her too. But I can never be angry with you. Just don't make her our friend,' said Prakash and followed suit.

I sat with Harsh and Prakash, but I exchanged the casual 'Morning' and 'Hi' and 'Bye' with Disha everyday. One day, I arrived late for my first lecture. I saw Disha. The seat next to her was the only vacant one.

Without looking at Harsh or Prakash, I sat next to Disha. After the first lecture ended, I got up.

'Where are you going?' she asked.

'I am sitting behind.'

'You won't be killed if you sit next to me for the rest of the day.'

I turned to look at Harsh and Prakash.

'I don't know if it is right,' I said.

'We are friends.'

To hell with it, I thought and sat next to her.

'You can talk to me if you want to,' she said.

She liked my company. I didn't mind being her friend.

The next morning, Harsh or Prakash didn't speak to me. When I entered the class, I saw Disha sitting alone in the classroom. If my friends wanted to act stupid, I couldn't help it. I sat next to her.

'Hi,' she said.

It was odd. I could smell the sweet fragrance of a perfume.

'I am glad you liked it,' she said.

'What are you talking about?'

'You know what I am saying. I am wearing it for the first time.'

She had never used a perfume before. I didn't understand what brought the sudden change.

'Are you going to sit somewhere else today?' she asked.

'No.'

For the next few days, I sat with her. Every day, I noticed a small change in her. After perfume, she wore earrings. Then, she changed her hairstyle. A fortnight later, Harsh and Prakash met me in the canteen. I was having my lunch alone as I had for two weeks.

'So, now you have cut us off?' asked Prakash.

'You both have cut me off,' I said.

'We are sorry,' said Harsh to me.

'Just because we don't like Disha, doesn't mean that you stop talking to us,' said Prakash.

'I will sit with her everyday. Is it a Deal?' I asked them.

'Deal,' they said and we shook hands.

So, I sat with Disha everyday and we three still talked to each other. The only condition was not to include Disha.

'You are nice to me. Why do people hate you?' I asked Disha, a few days later.

'I don't help or talk to anyone. That is why people perceive me as bad,' she said with a smile.

'Why not?'

'In my first semester, I wanted to top every exam. I paid heed to no one. By the time I realized that I had become unnecessarily competent, everyone stopped asking me for anything. They thought I was horrible. Since then, I didn't talk or help anyone.'

'Just try to talk or offer help to someone,' I said.

'I'll try,' she said as I stared at her.

One day, as I was heading back to the bus to go home, I met Girish.

'How was your result?' I asked him. The university results had come a day before.

'The internal marks dipped after my fight,' he said.

'You'll get better marks this semester.'

A boy came rushing up to him as students came out of the college building.

'Girish, I have to talk to you,' said the boy.

The boy took Girish aside and whispered something in his ear. Girish looked worried. The boy then rushed to the college gate.

'What happened?' I asked Girish.

'Manish, my classmate, went with me to the canteen yesterday with my other friends. He had a fight with a junior there. I had told him to cool down. Just now, Sarthak told me that he is going with few my classmates to beat up the junior, who is sitting in a bus in the parking lot.'

'Which bus?' I asked.

'790,' said Girish.

I knew someone in the bus.

'Disha!' I shrieked and ran.

'Stop Suhaas,' shouted Girish behind me.

I ran to the parking lot and saw the bus 790. A group of boys entered the bus and pulled out a boy sitting near the side window. The rest of the students ran down the bus. But the group of boys yanked the boy by his hair and threw him on the ground. The rest of the students stood there scared. Suddenly, many students ran towards the group from behind me and fought with the boy. More people joined the fight. It looked more like a war. I saw Disha. She stood in the midst of the fight. I tried to cut through the crowd and dodged the punches and kicks of students. Everyone fought with the person standing next to them without being sure of sides.

'Come,' I said as I reached Disha.

I held her hand and took each step.

'We are almost at the end,' I kept telling Disha as she shook with fear. I raised my neck and luckily saw Girish in the sea of humans.

'Girish,' I panted.

He held my hand and we crossed the sea. We finally came out of the hell.

We met Harsh and Prakash and told them what happened. The principal stopped the fight and rounded up Manish and his group.

Two days after the incident, Harsh and I were chatting in the classroom, when Prakash entered the class.

'Hi guys. I need to show you something,' he said.

He showed us a computer printout.

'Dance wiz?' I asked, looking at it.

'It is a dance fest on a single day. There are two events - Couple and solo dance,' said Prakash.

'We have to prepare a theory report for our fourth year project and we have job worries. No one has time for this. The dance event is after one and a half month,' I said.

'The new time table has arrived. We are going to have pre-placement periods for placement preparation. They are supposed to be periods when students can prepare for placement. The TPO couldn't arrange for any job material, so he asked all the HODs to make such a period. In short, we will have an hour free everyday. So we three can prepare for this dance fest without wasting time,' said Prakash.

'I don't like to dance,' said Harsh.

Prakash shifted his gaze towards me.

'No way, man,' I said.

'I was just offering help. If any of you wants to take part in this event, come to room 254 or the Cross Room in that period,' he said.

I wasn't keen on dancing. But, I thought of someone who could make use of it.

'Take part in the Dance Wiz,' I told Disha the next day.

We were in the library.

'Look. Right now you have a really bad image among other students. You need to look cool,' I said.

'I am not going to dance.'

'Not even for me?'

'If I'm a geek I don't mind it. I am not hurting anyone.'

I couldn't give up. I pressed on.

'Show that there is nothing wrong with you. Your only problem is that you have never scored in anything besides studies. At least, try.'

'I can't do it.'

It was time for plan B.

'I made a bet,' I said.

'What?' Disha asked.

'I made a bet with Harsh for 200 bucks that you can dance and he said you couldn't.

Please Disha, I'll lose the money,' I said.

It worked.

'I'll dance. But never make a bet like that again,' she grimaced.

Mission accomplished.

The next day, I went to the Cross Room during the Pre-Placement or PP period. It was the room from where an old professor had kicked us out during a play rehearsal.

'You stay outside the room,' I told Disha.

I told her that a student would teach her, but didn't reveal that he was Prakash.

'I am not going to teach that psycho geek,' boomed Prakash, when I met him.

'It is just a dance. What is the problem Prakash?'

'You remember Sapana?' he asked.

'The girl you dated with in the fifth semester and broke up in the sixth. You said things didn't work out between you two,' I said.

'I lied. We broke up as Disha said bad things about me to her friend, who passed it on to Sapana,' said Prakash.

'That is a lie.'

We looked on as Disha entered the room.

'This is pointless. I have nothing to do with any girlfriend of yours,' she said.

'You told her all the fibs.'

'Priya had told Sapana, who had spread all these rumors about me. But, I didn't bother much,' said Disha.

'I remember Priya. She is Simran's friend. After I broke up with Simran, she must have taken her revenge by breaking the bond between you and Sapana. You are my friend, after all,' I said to Prakash.

Prakash bowed his head in shame.

'I am sorry. I will certainly teach you from tomorrow,' Prakash said to Disha.

'I am doing it for Suhaas, otherwise I wouldn't care what you thought of me,' she said and left the room.

The next morning, I met Girish.

'Who are they?' I asked, as I looked at the three boys in the college ground.

They were playing cards.

'They are the worst boys in my class. They play cards most of the day. And, they always gamble with money,' said Girish.

'Who is that boy in the middle?' I asked.

'Som. He mostly wins among the three. He tries to talk to me, but I avoid him.'

I looked at Som, a guy with curly hair and a wild beard.

'Disha must go in for Salsa,' Prakash told me during the first lecture.

Harsh, who was sitting further down the row, was the only person amongst us, who hated Disha. I wanted to talk to Prakash about Disha's lessons.

'Isn't that a couple dance?' I asked him.

'Yes and you will be her partner.'

'You can't be serious,' I uttered in disbelief.

'You want Disha to have a cool image, so better help her out.'

'How do we learn Salsa in one and a half month?'

'You are not entering a Salsa competition. I can teach you the basics and a bit more.'

'Why don't you dance with Disha?'

'I am taking part in the couple dance. My partner is a second year girl and we will be practicing Waltz at my friend's home.'

He had pushed me into the crater as well.

'Tell her to wear high heel shoes for the dance from tomorrow,' Prakash said.

After the second lecture, I told all what Prakash had said.

'It is impossible,' said Disha.

'We will try' I said.

We met with Prakash and his partner in the cross room. Her name was Sonia. Her movements were more graceful as she moved to and fro from Prakash. Disha and I spent half an hour just looking at them.

'Slow down. Stop it,' I said.

Prakash switched off the C.D. player. He clasped his left hand with Sonia's left hand and put the other around her back. Prakash brought his left foot forward and she placed her right foot back. She placed her right foot forward and he placed his right foot back.

'These are the basic steps. For a whole week, just practice these. You both will have to practice at least two-three hours everyday,' said Prakash.

'We get only one PP period of one hour everyday. How will we find more time?' I asked.

'You will,' said Prakash.

From that moment, our dancing journey started. Prakash, Disha and I used every PP period and bunked every useless lecture. Disha did not like losing attendance, so we hit upon another idea. We told Vinay of the situation and asked him to cover two lectures in one and give every alternate lecture free. He also headed systems design lab and allowed us to finish our practicals and leave early in lab periods. We gained one and a half hour in that. So we used all possible time and Harsh never came to know a thing.

'Good,' Prakash said as he watched us rehearse a fortnight later.

The week before the sessionals, Disha and I had drawn the dance steps on paper and hummed and tapped our feet during lectures.

'It is wonderful. We are managing our reports and other jobs along with Salsa,' said Disha one Friday morning.

'Yes, me too,' I said.

I was nervous the first time I held Disha's hands and danced with her. She wore high heel shoes as suggested by Prakash. Disha had real problem the first three days, but she somehow got used to them.

'Next week we are having our sessional exams, so we can't practice,' announced Disha.

'Yes.'

'Why don't you include me in your project theory? All four of us will make the project the next semester,' she said.

'Harsh hates you and will never let you be a part of our group. He is in a foul mood and also has an assignment to finish,' I said.

Disha looked at Harsh. Then, back at me. She took her bag.

'What are you doing?' I asked.

'I'll meet you next week,' she said and left the first bench.

She told Prakash to go away and sat with Harsh. Harsh looked startled. Prakash came and sat with me.

'What happened?' I asked.

'She came and told me to sit with you.'

'I don't think she will practice today,' I said.

'She must be tired doing it everyday. You will practice with Sonia today.'

Sonia was an excellent dancer. I don't know why, but I didn't feel happy. I think it was so because she wasn't Disha.

The next week, Harsh met me after the second sessional outside the class, on Tuesday.

'How is the practice with Disha going?' he asked.

'You are not angry?' I asked.

'I am happy. Keep it up.'

That day, Disha sat with me. Prakash returned to his original seat.

'Are you going to sit with Harsh now?' I asked.

'No. I'll sit with you only.'

'How is Harsh so happy?'

'I helped Harsh in his assignment and told him about Salsa. He offered me to join the project group with you three,' she said.

'Why did you do it?'

'You told me to talk to people. I started with Harsh. He shouldn't hate me. He is your friend.'

Two weeks before the dance event, Disha was sitting with me in the embedded systems design lab.

'I won't be able to remember these programs. I don't know how I would pass the ESD lab,' she said.

'You will. We are going to cheat,' I declared.

'But how?' she was interested.

I remembered how Trisha helped me pass the Electronic Simulation External practical:

I couldn't mug up any programs. As soon as the exam started, I sat down to face a computer. Trisha sat next to me. She smiled.

'I have the programs, love. Switch on your mobile. And start your Bluetooth,' she said.

I knew what we were doing was illegal. Trisha transferred all the programs wirelessly to my cell phone. I opened the program that was assigned to me by the invigilator.

'Thank you,' I whispered.

'I will always do what I can for you,' she responded, before starting her own cheating.

'Can we really cheat?' Disha asked.

I returned to the present. I forgot that she volleyed a question.

'Yes,' I said. Every thought of Trisha was painful.

Disha and I spent every possible minute of the week for Salsa. We stayed late after college too. On Saturday, Prakash, Sonia, Disha and I went to Prakash's place.

'Disha is trying very hard, just for your sake,' said Prakash.

'What do you want to say?' I said.

'She has done everything to look attractive in your eyes. She uses perfume, dawns skirts. Damn it, she loves you.'

'Maybe.'

'Don't you love her too?' asked Prakash.

I didn't know the answer.

But, I said 'No.'

It was the last week before the Dance Wiz. On Monday, I felt ecstatic that I and Disha had done a reasonably good job at Salsa. My elation died when I saw Disha crying outside our classroom before the first lecture.

'What happened?' I asked.

'You know that we have to submit our bus fees by today, right?' she said.

'Yes, I know. I brought it today,' I said.

She narrated her story.

'I missed my college bus today and I took the Safdarjung-Gurgaon bus. My bus fee is Rs. 15000 and out of that I had kept Rs. 5000 separately in my pocket. As soon as I got down the bus, I checked my pocket. The poly bag was gone. I had been robbed.'

'I am so sorry.'

'My mother will ask tonight where the money disappeared. I won't be able to face her,' cried Disha.

'Stop crying. Go back to the class. No dance practice today. I will try to borrow money from someone,' I said.

She went back to the classroom. I sat in the canteen. Girish was already there.

'Bunking lectures?' I asked.

'I am in no mood to study.'

'Girish, I want your help,' I said.

I narrated Disha's story to him.

'I have Rs. 6000, but I had borrowed it and have to give someone by the end of the day. I already gave my bus fee. The only way to generate such an amount would be by gambling,' said Girish.

An idea struck my mind.

'I want to play cards with Som,' I said.

'I wasn't serious about gambling.'

'But I am ,' I said.

'What money do you have?'

'My bus fee.'

'You are crazy. If you lose the money, how will you pay the fee?' he asked.

'Right now, all I care is that Disha gets back her lost money.'

Girish scratched his chin. He looked at me seriously.

'You saved her in the parking lot fight. Today, you want to bet your own money to pay her fee. How much does she mean to you?'

Girish's question was tough. I could not see Disha in tears.

'She is worth everything I have,' I said.

'I'll play with you. We both will act independent but if I win, I will give you the profit apart from the Rs.6000 I have to give. If we lose, well, I will give you whatever money is left with me,' he said.

'Don't lose your money for me.'

'Don't be stupid. How many times have you played card games before? I play them all the time in the bus.'

Som sat alone in the college ground. He told us to meet after two hours and met us before the start of the third lecture.

Two boys came and said 'Hi' to Som. They saw us playing and asked to join in. They were not from mechanical as Girish did not know them. The betting game started. Som declared that we would play flash or *teen patti*. I don't remember their names so I will call them X and Y.

'What are the rules of this game? I have no idea,' I said to Som.

'In this game, the dealer distributes the cards and each player gets three. A set of three cards is called a 'hand'. There are different categories of *hand* and a higher ranking hand beats the lower ranking hand. There is this *pot*. The pot is the money or boot placed at stake by all the players. Initially, a boot is placed by all the players. As the game progresses, on his turn the player places either an equal amount of the bet that is on or raises the stakes. Everyone else has to chip in the amount accordingly,' explained Som.

'A player can ask a previous player to show his cards. The higher ranking hand will win and other player will pack up and leave the game. If a player is not confident of his cards, he can pack at anytime. In the end, two players are left. If one of them packs, other wins. If they both 'show', the higher rank wins. The winner takes it all,' added X.

'What is the ranking of hands?' I asked.

'The top hand is a trail - three of same cards. Highest combination is three aces and lowest is three twos. Then is the straight flush- having three consecutive cards of same suit. Highest is A-K-Q and lowest is 4-3-2. Then comes the sequence, which is same, except the three consecutive cards are not of the same suit,' said Y.

'Then we have the colour-having three cards of the same suit. Highest is A-K-J. Then comes the pair with two cards of the same rank, highest being A-A-K and lowest being

2-2-3. The lowest rank is the one, when none of the above combinations exists,' rounded up Som.

In the first game, Som dealt the cards and X sat to his left. Girish sat on Som's right. After Girish, Y sat and then me. The betting was anti-clockwise and the order was Girish, Y, me, X and Som. We all saw our hands. I got a pair of J-J-2. I placed Rs. 200. In the second turn, Som raised the stake by 100 i.e. Rs. 300. I placed 300. I asked for 'show' in the third turn. Y had Q-Q-3, a higher pair. I lost Rs. 500. By the fourth game, I lost Rs. 2500. I observed three things. The order of our seating always remained the same. Som crossed his hands after shuffling the cards and after a few seconds, showed them and distributed. Before every game, X went to the loo. It somehow seemed strange.

Before the fifth game, Som explained about the term *blind.* The person who played blind was not supposed to look at his card. No one could ask for show with any blind player. Everyone else except the blind players was supposed to give twice the amount the first blind player had declared. One player could play blind a maximum of two times. The third time, he had to see his hand.

Som told us how the game would progress.

'Now, we will all place our past winnings in the pot. Whoever wins this game, wins the pot. '

I hadn't won a single game so I watched the others as they placed the money. Girish's luck was bad. He too had lost Rs. 2500. But we had a chance to win back all our money.

'I'll play blind,' said Som.

Just then, a boy came running towards us.

'Som, the Fluids Motion professor wants to talk to you. Come quick,' he said.

'I'll come after some time,' Som said and left us.

X and Y also left. Girish and I went to the toilet on the ground floor.

'Why does X always come here before a game?' I asked Girish.

'I know. Som is always the dealer. He crosses his hands after shuffling. The order never changes. It is all fishy.'

'Why is Som playing blind?' I asked.

'Any one can,' said Girish.

'Think about it. The pot is huge. Would you trust your luck so much that you would play blind?'

'It's as if he knows that his luck is strong,' said Girish.

We stared at each other.

After forty-five minutes, Som returned. X and Y also reappeared.

'Just a minute,' X said predictably and went to the toilet.

After he came back, Som distributed the cards.

'I am playing blind too,' said Girish.

Som seemed disappointed.

'Is there any problem?' asked Girish.

'No,' said Som.

'Rs.500,' said Girish and placed the money on the table.

Som and Girish each gave Rs.500. Rest of us gave Rs.1000. Then Girish raised the stakes to Rs. 1000. He and Som gave Rs. 1000. X and Y packed. I placed Rs. 2000. Only three players were left - I, Girish and Som. It was the turn of both the blind players to see their cards. Girish opened his cards and looked at them.

'Pack,' he said.

'Are you sure?' asked Som.

'I don't think they are good enough.'

I and Som were the only people left.

I placed Rs. 2000.

'Here,' said Som and took out Rs. 4000.

He didn't look at his cards.

'Your blind is over. You should see your cards,' I said.

'I trust my fortune, your turn,' he said.

I didn't have Rs. 4000. I borrowed Rs. 2000 from Girish. His Rs. 6000 were finished. My bus fee of Rs. 10000 was gone.

'Show,' I said.

Som saw his cards. The colour drained off his face.

'Please,' I said.

Som looked wide eyed at his cards. He placed them down.

He had a straight flush consisting of K-Q-J of diamonds. I showed him mine.

'A-A-A. Trail of Three aces. One of diamond, one of Heart and one of spade. I win'

Som was shocked. He stared at me as I collected the money and stuffed it in my jacket and jeans pockets.

'This is impossible,' said Som. X and Y looked stunned as well.

'It wouldn't have been. If you had not rigged the game,' I said.

Som, X and Y watched me in fright. Girish understood what I meant. I addressed Som.

'I know you and your two friends here schemed this. I talked to Girish about it in the ground floor toilet. X went to the toilet many times. We suspected X for hiding something and searched the toilet. We found a bag in the small cupboard below the wash basin. After we opened it, we found nine decks of cards.

Each deck was kept in a cover that was named as a Deck with a number. Deck 0, Deck 1, Deck 2, Deck 3 had 'used' written on them. Deck 4 was missing. We understood that every game was rigged. In the first game, you had Deck 0. X went to the toilet, got the Deck 1 and sat beside you. You shuffled cards of Deck 0, crossed your hands and X took it and gave you Deck 1. It was the deck that was arranged the way you wanted, similar to Decks 2 to 8. After the fourth game, Deck 4 was with you, but you were away. Deck 5 was tucked safely in the bag. We knew the seating order.

So, we knew what our cards were supposed to be. You were supposed to have the trail of A-A-A, I was to have the trail of K-K-K, Girish was to have straight flush of K-Q-J, X was supposed to have the pair of 2-2-3 and Y to have a pair of 5-5-6. You wanted me and Girish to play and X and Y to pack soon. They would have to pay no money and we would be ripped off thinking we had a good hand. The pot would surely be distributed among you three.'

X and Y bowed their heads in shame. Som gulped.

'We rearranged the cards according to our needs. X and Y have the same cards you wanted. Girish has K-K-K. You know my and your cards. You were shocked that Girish packed. Even more surprisingly, I won with the perfect trail. You were so sure that you had my hand that you didn't see your cards after the blind was over. You wasted Rs. 4000 and lost all your money.'

Girish and I got up.

'You invested the two lectures scheming with X and Y after you met us. It was a great plan with a wrong approach,' I said.

Som got up and gathered the courage to fire back.

'You won't get away with this.'

I had only one answer.

'Som, if someone plays dirty with me, I return the favour.'

Girish and I walked and did not turn to look back at Som, X or Y.

'You are now his enemy,' said Girish.

I returned the money Girish had lost. I had got more than the Rs. 5000 that I wanted.

'So be it,' I replied.

After college got over, I met Disha. I gave her the Rs. 5000 and told her to pay the bus fee quickly. The next morning, I met her. I expected to see a smile on her face. But, she looked angry.

'Did you not pay the fee?' I asked.

'I did. But I know where it came from.'

Damn it! I thought. Who told her?

'I felt suspicious after I gave the fee. I asked Harsh and Prakash. They had been attending classes all day and said that knew nothing about it. I went to meet you in your bus. Harsh said you had left with Girish in an auto. I got Girish's number from Harsh and called him up. At first he was reluctant. Then he told me about your card games.'

'There was no other way.'

'I should have thrown the money in the dustbin.'

'No. I gambled because you needed the money.'

Disha looked at me with watery eyes.

'You are never gambling again for me. Promise me,' she said.

'I promise.'

The judgment day had finally come. I took out my shirt and trousers from the closet and tried them on. I was anxious to know what Disha was wearing. Prakash had become secretive towards me and so did Disha. They had decided what she would wear in the dance, but none of them told me. I took my cell phone and dialed Disha's number. It was switched off.

I called up Prakash.

'I thought you would pick me up. How will Disha reach college?' I asked him.

It was five in the evening. The function was to start at six and our performance was the second last in the couple dance. Prakash was at home. He had to pick me up from my bus stop and drive to college.

'Trisha is bringing Disha on her motorbike. Don't worry about her,' was the reply.

I waited at my bus stop. Prakash came in his car.

'Did you try to call Disha?' I asked.

'Her phone is switched off,' he said and started the car.

When Prakash danced on stage with Sonia, the crowd became

ecstatic. Prakash in his tux held Sonia firmly as she was led by him. They drifted from one corner to another gracefully. The audience cheered on.

I sat in the first row as I was one of the participants. Disha still hadn't come. I had not seen her even once since I stepped into college.

'That was a great performance,' exclaimed the announcer and Prakash and Sonia bowed to the audience and left the stage. I went backstage as the next couple was announced.

'How was our performance?' asked Prakash.

'Fantastic,' I said.

'Thanks,' said Sonia.

'Do you know where Disha is?' I came straight to the point.

'Yes, I met her half an hour before. I did her make-up and she had to change to her Salsa dress. Hasn't she met you till now?' said Sonia.

'No,' I replied.

'I am going to check her progress.'

'Please do,' I requested.

Sonia left.

'Are you nervous?' asked Prakash.

'Hell yes. The current performance will be over in fifteen minutes. Disha is not here yet,' I yelled.

'Be calm. She will be here in a few minutes,' he said.

Prakash took two chairs and sat next to me.

'Where is Harsh?' I asked.

'In the audience,' said Prakash.

Prakash went to meet Harsh. After ten minutes, Disha appeared backstage. At first I didn't recognise her.

'Suhaas?' she asked.

She looked like the most beautiful woman in the world. She wore no glasses. Her long hair fell to her arms. She wore a Latin halter red salsa dress. It appeared a one piece affair from the front that extended up to her knees. The hem of the bottom was spiral and asymmetrical. The top of the dress had a huge V cut so much so that I could clearly see her cleavage. As if it was not enough, she turned her back to me to talk to Sonia who had just come. I gasped.

Her dress was backless and was held by a single spaghetti strap. Below her waist was the skirt whose border could be seen. It was the most sensuous dress I had ever seen in my life. I felt hot. She turned to face me. There was a twinkle in her eyes that I had never witnessed before.

Was this the countenance that launched a million ships?

'Are you okay?' she asked.

'I am perfectly fine,' I said, wiping the sweat off my face.

'Prakash chose this dress. I know it is kind of revealing. But he said it was necessary.'

'What happened to your glasses?' I asked.

'Ever heard of contact lenses?' grinned Disha.

I was simply speechless and gawking at her like a zombie.

'Are you alright?' she asked.

'Nothing,' I said.

My temperature shot above 100 degree celsius, just by looking at her red dress.

'You'll be on the stage in five minutes,' Prakash cheered me as he came back.

'I have to go to the washroom,' Disha said and left.

'Haven't you seen a girl in a short dress?' asked Prakash.

'I felt odd seeing Disha in such a way,' I said.

Prakash laughed loudly.

'Why are you laughing?' I asked.

'I saw the look on your face. It happens when a guy sees a hot girl.'

'You changed her look. I seemed to be standing with some new girl in college.'

'Hi' said Disha as she reappeared.

'I'll be back' Prakash said and left us to think of our steps.

Maybe Disha could think, but I kept looking at her dress. To divert my attention, I looked at Prakash who was talking to a boy. The boy checked a list and parted the curtains and disappeared.

'Our next performance is Salsa. Wow. And to present this we have Suhaas and...' the announcer said and stopped midway.

He stared at the sheet and looked sideways at the boy. The boy nodded when the announcer whispered something. The announcer slowly declared to the clapping audience:

'To present we have Suhaas and Disha from ECE department.'

The audience stopped clapping and whispering began. 'Disha?' people asked each other. I became impatient. I motioned Disha to enter from the other side of the stage. I took a few deep breaths and walked in front of the audience. The audience clapped for me, unaware of what was to happen next.

'Where is your partner?' the announcer asked me.

Mouths fell open on seeing Disha walk in royally, with her head held high and extending her hand to me. People were astonished. She did not look like the Bookworm Disha. It wasn't just her outer beauty but her inner radiance. It was the confidence she exuded as she walked around me. The audience was hypnotized.

The truth was that I forgot my steps. Disha held both my hands and brought me closer to her. And the switch of my brain went 'on' and I remembered my steps. Thus, the salsa started. We stumbled a few times, but Disha covered each mistake quickly.

The boys wolf-whistled and the girls cheered on. Disha looked at me and smiled. What a reputation! The salsa had worked well after all. Disha had been wolf-whistled at for the first time in her life and that meant something. Salsa was not just some song and dance sequence. It was sheer magic as it portrayed love, despair, anxiety, loss, grief, relief. And, we expressed it all.

In the end, I pulled Disha towards me, and she fell into my arms. The crowd gave a standing ovation. Disha closed her eyes and panted. She had obviously enjoyed the dance, but she was tired.

'You were great,' I said.

'Thank you.'

At that moment, I knew what I wanted. If she was happy, I was happy.

We went to an empty classroom and sat there. Disha soon fell asleep. Prakash came after a few minutes.

'I and Sonia won the competition,' he said.

I congratulated him.

'I thought it would be both of you,' he said.

'Don't flatter me,' I said.

'I heard people raving about your performance. They were surprised with Disha.'

I nodded.

'Be careful now Suhaas. She's now a hot property. Every boy would love to date her,' Prakash said.

A few days later, Disha met me in the canteen, when I was talking to Prakash. Disha wanted to talk to me alone and Prakash headed for our classroom.

'Disha, what are you doing?' I asked.

'What?'

'Why couldn't you talk to me when I was standing with Prakash?' I asked.

'Well, I wanted to thank you in private. Everyone's been talking to me. Boys don't leave me alone. I told them only Suhaas will sit with me' she said.

'Disha, it was all okay before Salsa. But if we continue sitting together now, it will generate a gossip. People will think we are a couple. You should have a boyfriend.'

'You want to avoid me?'

'When did I say that?'

'You just did. This means you did everything for me to get rid of me. Boys would like me after seeing me in my Salsa dress. But no one was ever there to help me like you.'

'We are just friends.'

Disha didn't speak.

'What?' I asked.

'I thought we had become more than just friends. After all the time we had spent together,' she said and left the canteen.

I didn't sit with Disha after that. I went back to sit with Harsh and Prakash. For the first time in the four years of my college life, they sided for a girl. They rebuked me for letting Disha sit alone.

'You don't even feel bad. Wow,' Harsh expressed his sarcasm often.

November 21st was a Saturday, when Harsh called me in the morning. He told me that Prakash and Disha were at his home and helping him in the project theory. Disha had joined our project group

The 7th Semester ——————————————— 153

after Harsh's offer. I knew Harsh's real intention for calling me. He wanted me to talk to Disha.

When I reached his home, Prakash opened the door. He told that Harsh's mother had gone to the market. Disha was with Harsh in his room. I went up to Harsh's room. I opened the door and I saw Disha with him. Disha looked at me with surprise.

'You need help with the project theory?' I asked Harsh, completely ignoring Disha.

Disha left the room and headed for the kitchen.

'You know what I called you for. Stop acting ignorant and talk to her,' said Harsh.

I went to the kitchen where Disha was making herself a sandwich. She had her back turned to me.

'Disha, what is wrong? You don't talk to me. Why?'

Disha did not turn. But she spoke.

'You want to see me happy. Well, I am only happy with you.'

I became quiet.

'I have loved you since the day you joined college. Maybe some girls want a dashing, handsome, rich guy. I wanted a simple guy who cared for the people around him.'

Disha knew everything about me. I had never cared about her before that semester.

'When Trisha told me your story, I already knew all of it. When she broke up with you, I shouted at her for breaking your heart. She was confused with my reaction.'

Her voice was so loud that no one needed to eavesdrop.

'I had lost all hope of meeting you till the quiz happened. Fate wanted us to be together. When we kissed, I was on Cloud Seven.'

I felt guilty with every word that she uttered.

'You didn't know me. But you helped me with Salsa, you made me feel alive.'

Harsh sat on the sofa outside with Prakash.

'You rescued me in that parking lot. You risked your own money for me. I thought you felt something for me, Suhaas.'

At that moment, Girish also entered the scene. Disha took the plate in her hand.

'But do you know one thing? You are not supposed to do everything for me and still say you do not love me!'

She threw the plate on the floor which smashed into several pieces. One piece flew to her leg and brazed her knee but she stood firm. Finally, she looked at me. I moved closer to help but she pushed me away.

'Get away from me! I know you love me. I want you to know it and accept it. But you make me happy and push me away!' she shouted and picked up the broken pieces. Her hand started bleeding.

'Disha!' I shouted. I opened the tap and forced Disha to place her hand under the cold running water.

'It's only some physical pain. How does that affect me?'

'It's going to hurt a lot Disha! Put some damn cloth over the wound.'

'I don't care about you anymore! Fuck you,' Disha punched a hole in the air with her upturned finger and left the kitchen with her bleeding hand.

'Disha!' I shouted after her, but she left the house. Harsh raised his head slightly to see the open door. He closed it and sighed.

'Sit down Suhaas,' Prakash said.

'She's crazy,' I said.

'Calm down. Have some coffee.'

'No. Stop her. She's bleeding and she'll hurt herself.'

'Shut up!' Prakash said and passed me some coffee.

'She will probably go to Trisha and get herself bandaged. You can't go after her,' said Harsh.

'What can I do?' I asked.

'You do everything you possibly can for her. You do feel for her,' said Prakash.

I listened.

'That is how all boys are. We know when we are attracted to someone, but not when we truly love someone.'

'Can't we be just friends?' I asked.

'She doesn't want to be. You need to know why you care so much for Disha. You need to know if you love her.'

The month of November was the worst. I was doing okay in

academics. But I could not talk to Disha. She didn't talk to me at all. I concentrated totally on placement.

One day, I talked to my classmate Surinder from Gurgaon.

'I have a distant cousin, who was a farmer in U.P. before. You know how the rains are every year. Crop failure meant that he couldn't feed his family, let alone sell his crops. There was hardly any other employment in the village. He came to Delhi to earn money as a labourer. He wants to go back home, but he can't. He earns some money and sends whatever little he can, to his parents. Suhaas, life is hard for us. But it is much harder for the poor,' said Surinder.

In the last week of November, I talked to Vinay in his free lecture.

'Are you nervous about the placement?' he asked.

'Yes. The continuous pressure of getting a job is killing me besides one more thing,' I said.

'What is it?' Vinay asked.

'I will tell that another day,' I said. I didn't feel right, talking about Disha.

'Suhaas, do you really want to do a job? I saw the happiness in your eyes when you did the fourth semester project on your own. Would you not like to go for research and help someone rather than earn some profit for a company?' he asked.

It was a deep-rooted question.

'It comes to my mind. But, I have to earn for myself. How can I think about anything else?' I said.

'Don't ask me. Ask your heart,' he said.

December 1st. It was the day an I.T. major company named NewComp was recruiting students from various colleges. Our college was one of them. The venue for the exam was in a college at Faridabad. The recruitment had only two rounds. The written test and the interview. The recruitment was for all departments. So, Girish was eligible, along with Harsh, Prakash and I. I knew that if I had any luck, I might be able to scrape through the written test. All four of us hired a cab for the day. We left for the Faridabad College from Harsh's home.

'Are you nervous?' Harsh asked me in the cab.

'I am hopeful,' I said.

The written test started at 11 a.m. and lasted three hours. Luckily, the test had no major aptitude questions and there were no computer language questions.

'It was easier than the previous written tests,' said Prakash after the test.

'Certainly,' said Girish.

'Well, we have the cab ready if we have to leave early,' I said.

I had not seen Disha since we arrived at the Faridabad College. We sat down in the college auditorium. It was huge and comprised students from three colleges. Our own college, the host college and a third college.

After three painful hours, the T.P.O. stood with the company representative. Before declaring the result of the written test, the T.P.O. gave the exact number of students selected from each college. Our college list was the smallest, with 40 students, and the names of the selected ones were declared. I heard Disha's name. Harsh, Prakash and Girish were not on the list. The 39th name was that of Shashi.

'The names are in alphabetical order. Maybe your name is the last,' said Harsh.

'Let's go to the cab,' I said as I got up from my chair to leave.

'SUHAAS,' boomed the voice of the announcer in the auditorium.

I was stunned.

'Please, all the selected students come up here on the stage. Rest can leave,' said the curt company representative.

I watched the auditorium getting emptied. The selected students got on to the stage. The rest exited in a hurry, to go back home as fast as possible.

'You have been selected for the interview. Hurry man,' said Girish.

'Guys, where are you going?' I asked.

'We'll wait in the cab till your interview is over,' said Prakash.

I felt scared when my three friends left me. The auditorium was empty except for a handful of people. I went up the stage and saw the other students. I saw Disha standing alone in one corner. I wanted to stand by her side.

'Go to the Lobby Number 6. Your interview will be in room number 101,' informed the representative.

The room 101 was right in front of the lobby. It was transparent. It had glass doors and the interviewee could be seen answering the interviewer sitting across the desk.

There were six students before me and ten after me. My turn came after two hours. I was the seventh student to appear for the interview. I opened the glass door and asked the interviewer's permission. He called me in and asked me to sit.

'Please show your mark sheets and their photocopies,' asked the interviewer.

I gave my folder to him. He took out my resume and a red pen. He checked my strengths. He circled on creativity.

'What do you mean by that?' he asked.

I said I was creative as I always thought of new things. I said I was good at art, drawing cartoons.

'What is the difference between a cartoon and a portrait? Does some one need to look funny to draw his cartoon? ' he asked.

'No sir. Everything can be drawn in the way one wants. It is a matter of perspective,' I said.

I thought I could dodge the interviewer with heavy words. But he came up with more sublime questions. Then he asked about politics, to know my general awareness. I was confused if I was giving the interview for an I.T. company or a quiz.

'You can go,' he said finally and I left the room.

'Wait on the couch,' said the company representative, who sat in the lobby. After half an hour, he called me again. He took me outside the lobby and led me to another room.

'Go inside,' said the man and left. I opened the door and went inside. There was a man inside, sitting behind a desk. He offered me a seat.

'So, I have received the results of your first interview,' he said as he took out a sheet.

He looked young.

'Sir, did I do something wrong in the first interview? Is that why I have been summoned here again?' I asked, quite scared.

'Don't worry. We are making sure that we have the right candidate. I cannot tell you about your previous interview,' he said.

I felt hot around my neck.

'My name is Sirish, by the way,' he said and shook hands with me.

I felt more confident giving answers the second time. He asked about politics and general affairs, like the interviewer before. He asked some puzzles and calculations to be solved.

'I know that none of these questions have anything to do with software or computer languages. We want to see a student's attitude and presence of mind,' he said.

He came to the crucial question. And ,I was prepared for it.

'Why do you want this job and are you capable to do it?' he asked.

'Sir, I want to prosper and grow. I know your company and I can be a profitable asset.'

'You gave me a standard textbook answer. I've heard that many times,' he said.

I was lost. How could I say that I knew nothing of I.T. and I wanted the job badly? I could not tell him that there was a dearth of companies in my college.

'You like the I.T. sector?' Sirish asked.

'If your company finds me capable, then I'll start liking it,' I said.

Damn! What sort of answer was that?

'Would you be willing to do this job with all your heart, leaving apart the money?'

He had raised an important question.

'No,' was my answer.

Sirish was stumped. He looked me in the eye.

'What do you mean by that? You do not like this job?' he asked.

At that point, many people came to my mind. I remembered what Vinay had said to me about the project. I remembered Surinder, who had told about his cousin. Most unexpectedly, I remembered Simran's words.

'My aim in life, it is to give me the courage to achieve whatever aim I have at the present and not let it be decided by others.'

Sirish waited for my answer.

'I don't know if I would work with all my heart in your company or not. I haven't been there. But I know I want it,' I said.

'Do you hate this job?' Sirish asked.

'No sir. It's not your job sir. It's every job. If I work for a company, I work for its growth. I work for its profit. One of my professors made me understand and realize what I want. I worked on a simple project and that made me happy. Using my skills in helping someone would make me happy, even with lesser money,' I said.

'Who are you talking about? Explain to me,' Sirish said.

I told Sirish about Surinder's cousin.

'I sit here with you and am eligible for this job. But what about him? What did he do to deserve it? If I can do nothing to help him, what kind of an engineer am I?' I asked.

Sirish must have thought I was in a trance or sleep or something.

'Crores of people live in lakhs of villages. Most people, all young and old, have no work to do. Today, agriculture is unpredictable and farmers eat their own pesticides. Young boys go to cities in search of work and leave their families behind. Why should anyone leave their family behind?' I questioned Sirish.

I was in some strange mood. But Sirish took off his glasses and put them on the table. He listened patiently and so I continued.

'If I really am an engineer, then I can design products that can help in raising employment in villages and also in their progress,' I told.

'How?'

'If I am able to create a technology-based project that can be used in villages, I can generate employment. For example, if I make an electronic measurement machine that finds strength of materials like wood, bamboo, unwanted weeds and crop growth, I can develop cheaper houses for villages. If I develop solar or fuel cell based renewable energy generator, then I can generate continuous power for villages with sun and air as my inputs. There will be no input costs, only technological costs. Every product that I will create will employ millions. I will train the youth about the projects I build. Then, they will be able to make them on their own and sell them locally or to industries. Everyone will become self employed. Agriculture would become a luxury. No villager will have to go to the city to find work. If they do go, they would do so because they want to. Not because they have to.'

I thought I saw a tear run down Sirish's cheeks.

'Sir, I haven't thought of all these things all my life. But since I am unclear about a lot of things lately, I just said what I really meant.'

'It's a big dream. And sorry to say, it is far fetched and expensive,' Sirish said.

'I know sir. But I said all that because you asked me what I would do that would make me really happy, apart from money. Your company and sector are perfect. I believe you might have ten times better employees than me. But I want to research and develop things for the poor and I believe I am fit for your job. I will learn and implement everything you say. As for my interest, I need you. I need to become self-sufficient, gain experience and learn the ways of the world. Only when I gain confidence myself, I can provide it to others. Even if my dreams take another 20 or 30 years, I want to strengthen my own position now.'

Sirish didn't speak for a few moments after listening to me. He wore his glasses.

'You can go now,' he said softly.

At nine o' clock, I reached my cab. My friends were waiting there.

'What happened, why did you take the whole day? How was the interview?' asked Prakash.

Only when I came out of the college building, I realized what all I had said. Probably Disha's behaviour and Vinay's words had led to that breakdown. The pressure of job and process of lying had kicked the truth out of me.

'I think I screwed up,' I said and sat in the cab and told them the whole story.

The results were to be announced in the Faridabad college the very next evening. Prakash, Harsh and Girish accompanied me.

'I am not going to make it,' I said as we sat down in the auditorium, awaiting the outcome.

The company representative went up the stage. He read out the final names of successful candidates from our college.

Disha's name was not there. I wished it was.

'SUHAAS,' said the representative.

I sagged in my chair. My mind ran in frenzy as several hands extended to congratulate me. Only 16 students were selected from our college. Whether luck or not, I was one of them.

'Congratulations buddy,' said Girish, Prakash and Harsh in unison.

After all the names from all the three colleges were announced, everyone else left except Prakash, Harsh and Girish and I. The representative addressed us for twenty minutes.

'You all now belong to the New Comp Family. Welcome home,' he said finally.

When we four exited the college, the cold night air caught us unawares.

'I don't remember where the car is,' said Prakash.

'I'll go and check it out,' I said.

We were fools not to take the driver's number.

I went to the car parking and finally found the car and the driver sleeping in it. I called Prakash and told him. At that moment, someone called out my name. To my surprise I saw Sirish walk over to me.

'Hello' I said automatically.

'Congrats' he said.

'After what I said, I don't get why you would still want me.'

'Did you really mean what you said inside?'

'Yes sir. I need a job alright,' I said.

'I meant about helping villages.'

The moment he said it, there was a childish gleam in his eyes.

'Yes sir. I don't know when it would happen but yes I meant it.' I said.

'My father wanted to help those who were in grave need. He was a simple employee all his life. He couldn't do anything. I love where I am. But I couldn't ever do what my father wanted and never know if I will,' he said.

He talked to me like a friend.

'But after what you said, I think there are better people than me. If you meant everything you said, you deserve this post,' he said.

'But…' I began and he cut me short.

'I don't know what qualities you have, but you are eligible and a good person. I didn't give you the job because you needed one. But, because you deserved it. There is always a first step. This is yours. I have given you time to know the world better. I would hate it if you were not true to your word,' he said.

'I won't disappoint you,' I assured.

'It was my best interview' he said in return and bid me goodbye. He walked out of the parking lot and after a minute, a sea of students rushed in.

'Where were all you guys stuck?' I asked Prakash as he and Girish surfaced.

'The company representatives were leaving when they found one of them missing. The guy didn't even have a cell phone on him and we were told to search the college building for him. He just came out of the parking lot. Said that he thought his car was parked there. Weird guy,' said Prakash.

'I wish you three got selected,' I said.

'We'll surely get selected, someday,' said Harsh.

'But now you are employed and so it's the right time,' said Girish.

'What time?' I asked.

'Party time!' they all shouted together.

The three days that passed after that were full of celebrations. I found myself giving parties to all those who congratulated me. I wished Disha would come and ask for a party. But she didn't . I had wanted her to be selected for NewComp as well.

On Saturday, the 6th December, I went to the college. It was stupid to have a Saturday as a working day. Prakash, Harsh and Girish had not come. A good Telecom company was recruiting students on Sunday, all those scoring above 80% . As Disha was obviously eligible, she studied for the written test in the library. I decided to talk to her. I left for the library before the third lecture. As I entered the library, I saw her seated in the far corner near the window. I sat next to her.

She was immersed in the previous year papers of the company.

She didn't notice my presence. I touched her hand. Disha looked at me with surprise.

'What are you doing here?' she asked.

'I wanted to be with you,' I said.

'Just because you got a job, you have no right to interfere in my life and ruin my career as well,' she said.

'What can I say to make you happy?'

'I don't want to talk to you.'

When I headed to the college bus after the last lecture, I saw Trisha standing outside my bus.

'Were you bunking all day?' I asked.

'No. I was absent today. I just reached here to pick you up,' she said.

'Are you taking me to my home?'

'No. My apartment.'

'I don't want to come.'

I realized that I hadn't talked to her for six months.

'Don't make me beg. It is important,' she said.

'Fine,' I agreed and walked with her to the parking lot. I saw her motorbike.

'You drive the motorbike,' she said and gave me the keys.

'No way,' I resisted.

'I taught you how to ride it when we were a couple. Don't tell me you don't remember,' she said.

Trisha sat behind. It was strange. A year ago, I had wished that I knew how to ride the bike and wanted her to sit at the back. Now, when I was in the front seat, all those feelings that existed between us were gone. We reached her apartment and rang the bell. The door swung open to reveal Prakash.

'Hi Suhaas,' he said.

I was speechless.

'Hello,' said Girish and he came out of the kitchen.

I didn't know what to do.

'Let's go to my room,' Trisha said.

When we entered her room, I was shocked to see Harsh.

'I wanted some of metal band CDs that you have,' he said as he looked at her.

'Take whichever ones you want,' said Trisha.

'Fine. Oh, hi Suhaas,' said Harsh and left the room.

Trisha closed the door behind me. I sat on her bed and she sat on the chair next to the desk.

'What is happening? I thought Harsh hated you,' I said.

She could not just casually talk to my friends and then be cool about it all. She finally told everything.

'After I broke up with you, I thought a lot about my past. I went to my home and told my father how his actions had affected my nature. He apologized and loved me. He had changed. I stayed with my parents during the summer vacations.'

She paused and sat next to me. She continued.

'When I returned to college this semester, I wanted to talk to Harsh. In those two months I had spent with my parents, not once did I feel any violent streak. Disha had told me about the Salsa classes. So when you, Prakash and Disha went to practice, I sat with Harsh. He listened to me, but never said anything. Only after a month did he speak to me. He forgave me. But then Harsh told about you and Disha. He too had become Disha's friend. It was clear that you both love each other. You are still not ready to accept it. I waited whole November to hear from your friends that you said it. You did not. So I brought you and the gang here today. I want to know your answer.'

'What should I say?'

'If you were to choose between Disha and me, who would it be?' she asked.

Surprisingly, I could not say it to myself. But at that moment, I could easily tell it to Trisha.

'Disha,' I said.

'Do you love her?'

'Yes.'

'Then why not say it to her? Do you fear she will break-up with you?' asked Trisha.

'No,' I said, 'I thought at first she would ruin my life when she proposed to me. But as I got to know her, I wanted her to be happy. I love her. But I feel that our relationship will break if she stays with me, given my past.'

'Right now, you are the one who is breaking the relationship. Before you met Disha, every break-up had some reason that had nothing to do with you. Destiny wants you and Disha to be together. You can never be sure if your relationship will last for a lifetime. But you know that you both truly love each other. I am sure, she will be very happy with you.'

'She does not want to talk to me. She didn't listen to me today.'

'That was because you were not sure until now. Say it. She wants to hear it from you.'

As I got up to leave, I noticed something. A shirt was kept in a basket on the floor. It was the same Rock Band shirt I had given to her.

'I thought you said you hated that band and you said you would give it to someone,' I said.

Trisha snatched it from me and stared at me for a minute.

'Go Suhaas. Tell Disha your feelings as soon as possible,' she said.

I left the room and shut the door behind me. I saw Harsh, Prakash and Girish.

'Will you tell Disha that you love her?' asked Girish.

'Yes,' I said and they cheered.

As I left Trisha's apartment with others, I thought of the rock band shirt. I knew that when I had shut the door, Trisha was crying. I loved Disha. Disha loved me. But Trisha still loved me.

On 8th December, the Monday, I met someone whom I didn't want to. But it looked like life was coming back in full circle. When I sat in the college ground alone during lunch, Simran came and sat next to me. I couldn't ignore her. She didn't wait for me to talk and exploded.

'I am sorry. I know what I did was wrong. I thought of using your name just to get attention. Please be my friend and accept this locket,' she said.

She showed me her locket.

'Fine,' I said and took it.

'Are we friends?'

'I can't hate you forever.'

'Thanks,' she said.

'By the way, I remembered what you had said in Mr. and Mrs. Fresher contest, during my interview,' I said and told her about my interview with Sirish.

On 9th December, the next day, I met Vinay alone in his lab.

'I love Disha,' I said.

'How are you so sure?' he asked.

'It's like you said. Fate didn't want us to be apart. I screwed up everything. Though right now, she is not talking to me. What should I do?' I asked.

'On this Saturday, the college is arranging a function to honour third and fourth year students who got good marks in the last semester. I bet Disha will be awarded as she topped your department in the last semester. Maybe she will listen to you. It is your last chance before exams.'

'That is a great idea,' I said and got ready to leave the lab.

'Best of luck,' said Vinay.

I hugged him and he was surprised.

'You hugged me because I gave you the idea?' he asked.

'No. I remembered you during the interview. You showed me the right path,' I said and explained my interview with Sirish.

The D-day had arrived. The 13th December, Saturday is still etched in my mind. The air was cold and I felt the tension inside. It was good as after that all the students had to only appear for exams. The function was to take place in the evening. But as most of us commuted by buses, we were dropped in the college around 3 p.m.

'You are going to tell her today, right?' asked Harsh.

'Yes,' I said.

'Please do,' said Prakash.

The function was to be held in the college ground. A proper wooden stage had been prepared for the first time. Its ceiling was supported by four wooden pillars and several wooden crossbeams. It was huge and magnificent. We all were supposed to sit in wooden chairs under a flat cloth canopy tent, also supported by wooden pillars. It had a curtain each on the left as well as on the right side. The back side of the tent was the exit. The front side was to view the stage. The wooden stage also had curtains on the left and right. It was a royal setting.

Around 5 p.m., I was surprised to see Aakriti arrive with Jaggu in tow. I met them.

'Wow, how are you here?' I asked.

'A professor invited me. I brought Jaggu as well,' said Aakriti. Jaggu smiled. I had helped them in coming together, after all.

'Please be seated,' I said.

Soon after them, the whole tent got occupied. Aakriti and Jaggu sat in the first row with the professors and other staff. I sat with Harsh, Prakash and Girish. I looked around for Disha, but she was nowhere to be seen. I found Trisha in the row ahead of me.

'Have you seen Disha?' I asked.

'No, I think she might be in the front row. She is going to be awarded today anyway.'

I went back to my seat and waited patiently for her. An hour passed but Disha did not appear on stage. A fashion show took place for which an inclined ramp was built from the wooden stage to the ground inside the tent. I hated the thin stream of carpet that covered the stage, the ramp and the ground. A chief guest was invited who ignited the *deepshikha,* a three feet brass candle stand that had a provision for fifteen oil candles. The chief guest slowly ignited each oil candle (*diya*), which stood near the curtain and smiled at the audience.

I had enough of the rubbish. For another hour, no award presentation happened. Even a musical *kawwali* took place. The first and second year students sang in full throttle as they sat on cotton mattresses. When the *kawwali* ended, no one cared to remove the mattresses.

The announcer came and kicked aside one of the mattresses such that it slipped on the ramp. I had failed to understand if it was a function to honour meritorious students or was it an entertainment fiesta. The chief guest was invited to say a few words and I left the tent.

I entered the college building and walked to the water cooler on the ground floor.

I had just quenched my thirst when I heard an announcement. The meritorious students were being called on stage. I headed for the exit of the building. But then, I saw a burly fellow in the corridor whom I didn't want to. He was with his two usual friends.

'Suhaas!' said Som as he came near.

'I am surprised too. I have to go,' I said.

'Hey, you robbed me of my money. You hurt me. I should return the favour.'

'Absolutely,' said his friends.

Som and his friends blocked my path.

'I will give you all the money you want. Just leave me for now,' I said.

'Money won't help.'

Som punched me in the ribs. He and his friends took turns to batter me as I fought alone. When Som threw me on the ground, a group of boys entered the building.

'Hey, he is the leopard boy! He is in trouble,' shouted one of them who saw me. They all rushed to my aid.

They were six juniors who grabbed Som and his friends by their collars.

'Go!' shouted the boy to me, as they beat the hell out of Som and his friends.

'Thanks,' I said and rushed to the exit. The names were being called out.

'The last name is Disha,' said the announcer.

When I entered the tent, I saw the chief guest give Disha a certificate. He placed a golden medal around her neck.

'Disha recently got placed in the prestigious telecom company *Vayucel*. We request her to say a few words about her achievement,' said the announcer.

With that, the announcer gave her a cordless mike and he and the chief guest left the stage. I only walked a few rows further when a mishap happened.

A strong wind caused the wooden stage curtain to strike the *deepshikha*. The *deepshikha* got caught in the curtain and the curtain caught fire. It fell on the stage carpet and the carpet caught fire as well. Everyone ran towards the exit. Pandemonium reigned.

Chairs fell down as people ran helter-skelter. I could not think of anything as my ears pained with the loud screams. I closed my eyes in fear.

'Suhaas, come out,' shouted someone.

As a stream of rushing students headed towards me, a hand knocked me and I fell to the ground. I had suffered enough pain.

'Help,' I heard a distant cry.

I looked up at the stage. I saw Disha shouting, hanging by a crossbeam in the ceiling.

'I am coming,' I said and got up on my knees as my body writhed in pain.

Suddenly, a hand grabbed my collar and dragged me out of the tent. Girish, Trisha, Aakriti, Simran, everyone I knew in my college life, stood at the exit.

'Do you want to die?' asked Harsh, as I looked at the person who had grabbed my hand.

'Disha is in there!' I shouted at him.

Trisha came running to me.

'Take this. Save Disha,' she said and removed her jacket.

'Take these,' said Aakriti, as she stuffed Jaggu's motorbike gloves into my hands at the same time.

'Go!' Everyone shouted.

I ran as fast as I could. I saw the mattress on the burning ramp and walked over it. I looked at Disha hanging above.

'Let go!' I shouted.

'I don't want you!'

'I want to kiss you, for real this time.'

As soon as I said that, she let go of the crossbeam and fell into my arms.

'Let's scoot,' I said and ran over the mattress. The crossbeams fell behind me and the entire stage crumbled. I avoided the burning wooden pillars that fell with flames all around me. My jacket caught fire as I came out of the falling tent. Someone splashed cold water on me from behind and I was all wet. I let go of Disha and Harsh removed my jacket.

A cloth was patted against my back forcefully and recurrently.

'You will be all right,' said Anu as she patted my back with a cloth in her hand.

'He is fine. You extinguished the fire on the coat,' shouted Harsh.

'There are just minor burns,' said Prakash.

Trisha gave me a small towel to dry my hair. I observed as Anu walked towards Prakash.

'Thanks for helping Suhaas,' said Prakash.

'I wanted to apologise,' she said.

'Such a beautiful setting razed to the ground,' said a professor as the stage disintegrated, the fallen canopy looked like a white flaming ghost and the wood burnt like bonfire.

Prakash and Anu talked to each other. Everyone else was busy helping other students bring water from inside the college building and extinguishing the fire. No one was looking at me. I walked over to Disha and took her away from the crowd, under a tree.

'Look, I love you. There are no two ways about it. If things go bad, at least it won't be my fault,' I said to her.

'Good. I still can't believe you came to save me.'

'So, what about my reward?'

'What reward?'

'Well, I said I wanted to kiss you and I meant it. What about that?'

'Later.'

'The girls I met before you are far better kissers. I don't even need your kiss.'

She looked affronted. But that did the trick.

'Other girls might be better in many ways. But no one would love you more than this geek goddess,' she pouted.

She moved closer and we kissed passionately. It was just what I wanted.

A perfect ending to The Seventh Semester.

❑

Epilogue

'That's it?' asked the girl.

It was eight p.m. Suhaas had told his story despite continuous interruptions. At seven p.m., when Harsh, Prakash, Girish, Trisha and Disha had arrived, he evaded them as he was quite miffed with them for coming late. He was astonished at the girl's statement at that moment.

'What do you mean by that?' asked Suhaas.

'You told me the story till the seventh semester. Why not the eighth?'

'The seventh semester is special to me. My love and career life came one full circle. Still, I can tell you what happened in the eighth semester.'

'Yeah. Did your friends find their partners?'

'Anu changed a lot after she apologized to Prakash. And now, they form a happy couple. So do Girish and Trisha. Trisha and Girish have same levels of temper – fire for fire.'

'What happened with Disha and her father?' asked the girl.

'She did what Trisha did. She called up her father and gave him a mouthful. Her dad realized what he lost and apologized to his daughter. He didn't leave his second wife, but allowed Disha to meet her step sister and they have talked frequently in the eighth semester.'

'What about the job situation?'

'Recession hit our college like the rest of the country. Lesser companies came, and some already-selected students were rejected or their joining got postponed. Girish got a job in a good mechanical company. Trisha got a job with a small firm. Prakash was also offered a job, but he preferred to study for higher education, like M.Tech or MBA. He'll figure a way out. Anu too got a job in some I.T. company.'

'What happened to that dream of yours that you told the interviewer?'

'Well, I made the fourth year project with Harsh, Prakash and Disha. It was much better than the magic wand and brought me closer to my dream. Right now, I got to concentrate on my job, not experiment any more.'

'You completely missed out on Harsh,' she said.

'Harsh loved only Nishi, who quit college after the second semester. He was never interested in any other girl. A telecom company has selected him for an interview, which is two days later. He needs something more than his friends to cheer him up – some silver lining to brighten his day.'

A beep sounded on the girl's cell phone. She checked it and kept it back in her pocket.

'I have a good news to brighten up Harsh,' she announced.

Suhaas looked baffled.

'Anu really changed after she apologized to Prakash. She tracked down Nishi. Actually, Nishi's cell phone had got stolen when she left this college after second semester. She didn't have any contacts and Anu had broken friendship with her, so she couldn't call her. Anu met Nishi a week back and gave her Harsh's contact number. She also gave a photo of Harsh and his friends.'

'Who are you?' asked Suhaas, totally confused.

'I am Nishi's friend. She gave me that photograph and I knew who you and your friends were, before meeting you. I expected Nishi to reach this college by three, but found you instead. I wanted to know about Harsh and his friends. Nishi just messaged me that she *is standing outside the college gate. If only Harsh would meet her now, she could say sorry for losing contact.'*

Suhaas spotted Harsh and told him about the girl and Nishi. Harsh rushed out of the college gate and the girl picked up her purse and walked towards the exit.

'Hey, what's your name?' shouted Suhaas.

'It doesn't matter. My work is done,' she said, walking out of the door.

'Wait. What about your story?' asked Suhaas.

The girl smiled.

'Not tonight. But I bet it's better than yours.'

With that, she opened the gate and vanished into the blue. Suhaas was all alone, with only the image and voice of Nishi's friend on his memory screen. He was keen to meet her, soon.